Mai Sakurajima

Third-year at Minegahara High. Very busy—and very famous—actress, but also Sakuta's girlfriend.

And his sister,
steels hers[e]
a big ste[p]

She'd spent a long time at home alone.
And now she's braving the outside world again, w[...]

Rascal
DOES NOT DREAM
of a
Sister
Venturing
Out

Hajime
kamoshida

Illustration by
keji mizoguchi

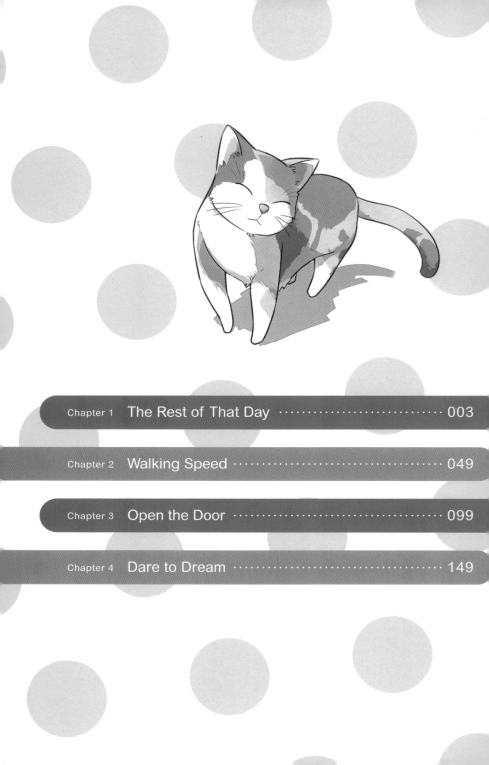

Kaede,
lf to take
into the future.

earing the coat Mai had given her to the nurse's office at school.

Sakuta Azusagawa

Unconventional second-year student who doesn't even have a cell phone. The rumor mill turned him into a bit of an outcast.

After lots of tears and lots of help, normal life has returned. As the third term begins, everyone has to choose a future.

Even as Mai's time with Sakuta at school draws to a close, there are moments of joy to be found.

Rascal
DOES NOT DREAM
of a Sister Venturing Out

HAJIME KAMOSHIDA

Illustration by
KEJI MIZOGUCHI

New York

Rascal Does Not Dream of a Sister Venturing Out
Hajime Kamoshida

Translation by Andrew Cunningham
Cover art by Keji Mizoguchi

SEISHUN BUTA YARO WA ODEKAKE SISTER NO YUME WO MINAI Vol. 8
©Hajime Kamoshida 2018
Edited by Dengeki Bunko
First published in Japan in 2018 by KADOKAWA CORPORATION, Tokyo.
English translation rights arranged with KADOKAWA CORPORATION, Tokyo through
TUTTLE-MORI AGENCY, INC., Tokyo.

English translation © 2022 by Yen Press, LLC

Yen On
150 West 30th Street, 19th Floor
New York, NY 10001

Visit us at yenpress.com
facebook.com/yenpress
twitter.com/yenpress
yenpress.tumblr.com
instagram.com/yenpress

First Yen On Edition: August 2022
Edited by Yen On Editorial: Ivan Liang
Designed by Yen Press Design: Andy Swist

Yen On is an imprint of Yen Press, LLC.
The Yen On name and logo are trademarks of Yen Press, LLC.

Library of Congress Cataloging-in-Publication Data
Names: Kamoshida, Hajime, 1978– author. | Mizoguchi, Keji, illustrator.
Title: Rascal does not dream of bunny girl senpai / Hajime Kamoshida ;
illustration by Keji Mizoguchi.
Other titles: Seishun buta yarō. English
Description: New York, NY : Yen On, 2020. |
Contents: v. 1. Rascal does not dream of bunny girl senpai —
v. 2. Rascal does not dream of petite devil kohai —
v. 3. Rascal does not dream of logical witch —
v. 4. Rascal does not dream of siscon idol —
v. 5. Rascal does not dream of a sister home alone —
v. 6. Rascal does not dream of a dreaming girl —
v. 7. Rascal does not dream of a girl and her first love —
v. 8. Rascal does not dream of a sister venturing out —
Identifiers: LCCN 2020004455 | ISBN 9781975399351 (v. 1 ; trade paperback) |
ISBN 9781975312541 (v. 2 ; trade paperback) | ISBN 9781975312565 (v. 3 ; trade paperback) |
ISBN 9781975312589 (v. 4 ; trade paperback) | ISBN 9781975312602 (v. 5 ; trade paperback) |
ISBN 9781975312626 (v. 6 ; trade paperback) | ISBN 9781975312640 (v. 7 ; trade paperback) |
ISBN 9781975312664 (v. 8 ; trade paperback)
Subjects: CYAC: Fantasy.
Classification: LCC PZ7.1.K218 Ras 2020 | DDC [Fic]—dc23
LC record available at https://lccn.loc.gov/2020004455

ISBNs: 978-1-9753-1266-4 (paperback)
978-1-9753-1267-1 (ebook)

1 3 5 7 9 10 8 6 4 2

LSC-C

Printed in the United States of America

Looking back, things were already in motion.
By the time I noticed, it was *real*.
And because I noticed, it was almost gone.
Before that, it had been in a box, its state unknown.
I had to open it to see inside.
Everything that really matters works like that.
Like Schrödinger and his cat.

тне rest of тнat Day

1

Sakuta Azusagawa was dreaming.

He was standing alone on the beach at Shichirigahama, staring out at the sea.

It was all a bit off—he could smell the salt in the air but couldn't hear the wind or the surf.

The colors weren't quite right, either. The sea should've been a deep blue and the sky a lighter shade, but these colors were far too pale.

And that was how he knew he was dreaming.

He looked left and right and saw no one on the shore. No windsurfer's sails on the water ahead.

He had it all to himself.

But even as that thought crossed his mind, he heard someone walking on the sand, trailing a red scarf as they slipped past him.

A little girl with a red leather backpack.

She went down to the surf, standing just beyond the wave's reach.

Beautiful, perfectly straight, shoulder-length black hair. The backpack looked brand-new, with not a scratch or stain on it.

She was probably six or seven years old.

Sakuta didn't know her.

But he'd caught a glimpse of her face as she walked past, and it had reminded him of someone.

Had he seen her somewhere before?

They hadn't properly met. Sakuta didn't know anyone her age.

But he felt like he should.

A gust of wind whipped her hair around, and Sakuta's jaw dropped.

He *had* seen her before. They'd never spoken, but he'd placed her now—she was on TV all the time. Everyone knew the famous child actress.

"Mai...?"

The name came unbidden.

She turned around at his call. There was a defensive look in her eyes. They gave him a once-over. This was exactly how the modern eighteen-year-old Mai Sakurajima would have acted.

"Who are you, mister?" she asked, her tone bright and childlike.

To a kid her age, high school students clearly counted as "grown-ups."

"I guess I've got one foot in that door..."

"My mom said I'm not supposed to talk to strangers. Sorry!"

She bobbed her head politely and turned her back on him.

"Where's your mom?"

It was just the two of them here.

"......"

She'd heard him but wasn't answering, apparently pretending not to hear.

"You alone?"

"......"

Her mother's rule had to be observed. She'd been looking west at Enoshima, but when she turned east toward Kamakura and Hayama, he caught a glimpse of a frown.

He looked left and right himself. The beach was still deserted. Only him and the girl in the backpack stood on the sand.

"Are you lost?"

"?!"

Evidently, yes.

"No!" she said, glaring at him. That same grumpy glare modern Mai often gave him.

And that made him break out in a smile.

"Where is this?" she asked, like she took issue with that grin.

"I thought you couldn't talk to strangers."

"……Fine, then."

Even grumpier. She turned her back on him again and started walking toward Enoshima.

"You're on Shichirigahama," he called after her.

She stopped.

He waited till she turned back, then added, "But actually, it isn't even *one ri*."

"……"

Her lips didn't move. She just looked right at him, not saying a word.

"I go to school here. Minegahara High. Name's Sakuta Azusagawa."

He pointed up at the school building, belatedly introducing himself.

"Now I'm not a stranger, right?"

She blinked, eyes wide…but surprise soon gave way to a smile.

Her lips moved. He assumed she said something.

But he couldn't make it out.

"Azusagawa!"

A different voice roused him from the dream…

"Azusagawa! Wake up!"

He raised his head and found his English teacher glaring down at him, more fed up than mad.

"Good morning," Sakuta said. Seemed like the right thing to say.

But it earned him a dramatic sigh.

"Never mind. Kamisato, you read for him."

The teacher left Sakuta's window-side desk and headed back toward the blackboard.

"Huh? Why me?"

Saki Kamisato sat next to him and did not appreciate the fallout.

"Blame Azusagawa," the teacher said.

She clearly did. Sakuta pretended not to notice her glare and did his best to nonchalantly turn to look out the window.

The waters of Shichirigahama lay before him—the same location as in his dream. It was just past three PM. The sun was descending across the sky to the west, and the navy-blue waters sparkled in its light. The sky was clear and blue, and the line of the horizon seemed to glow with an almost mystic light.

These colors had been dulled in his dream, but here they were vibrant.

A sight for sore eyes.

Perfect for absent gazing.

In mid-January, the air was clear, and he could see for miles.

Soaking in the twin blues of the sky and the sea, Sakuta mulled over his dream. He'd been dragged out of it at an awkward moment, and he was curious what would have happened next.

What had young Mai been about to say?

He considered going back to sleep, in the hopes of finding out, but before his head went down, the teacher caught his eye…and he was forced to abandon the idea.

"Well, it was just a dream."

Propping one cheek up on his hand, he let his eyes drift to the window once more. Saki Kamisato was reading aloud, totally nailing it—but he could hear the irritation building in her voice.

She was pretty much always mad at him, though. He didn't have it in him to care.

And not long after, the bell rang. End of sixth period.

"Rise! Bow."

And the classroom crowd dispersed in a flurry of good-byes and see-ya-laters.

Classmates rushing off to clubs or practice. Students on cleaning duty begrudgingly grabbing brooms.

Sakuta had no reason to linger, so he booked it before Saki Kamisato could drag him aside for a scolding. He thought it best to keep his distance when furious women were around.

"Azusagawa."

A teacher caught him in the hall. It was Class 2-1's homeroom teacher, a man in his midforties.

"Yeah?"

"You know you still haven't turned in your survey. At least get it to me Monday."

"Sure."

"You are not inspiring hope here."

He started to rap Sakuta on the head with the attendance file but then thought better of it. Teachers couldn't exactly dish out corporal punishment these days.

"I'll try not to forget."

"Then *don't* forget!"

"Okay."

Sakuta said the right thing and headed for the stairs. He heard the teacher yelling "Please!" behind him, but he ignored it. He had to get out of here before Saki Kamisato caught up with him. She could be a real pain.

His class was on the second floor, so he headed down.

His mind was now on the survey…and his plans for the future.

It wasn't worth fretting about. He'd already made up his mind to go to college and had narrowed that list down to a pair of prospects.

There were two big problems, though. One was Sakuta's own academic performance. This, he would have to solve by hitting the books real hard.

The other was financial. He had yet to tell his parents about any of this.

If they'd lived together, he might have had a chance to bring it up or maybe someone would have even asked him first. But then his sister got bullied at school, and fallout from that had eroded their mother's confidence as a caretaker, leaving her in a frayed state of mind. They now lived separately.

Their father was looking after their mother while covering Sakuta and Kaede's living expenses. They'd been like that for two years.

Sakuta would rather not be a burden on his father any longer. Public colleges might be cheaper than private ones, but they certainly weren't free.

He was sure his father was thinking about the problem, too. They needed to sit down and talk, but with one thing and another, they hadn't found the time. And that was why the survey was sitting in his bag, still blank.

"But the studying is probably the bigger challenge."

Financing didn't matter if he couldn't pass the entrance exams. He'd have to do the work first.

And he could always turn in the survey next week. No matter what problems lay ahead, giving up on college was no longer an option.

She wanted to go there with him.

A request from the cutest girl in the whole wide world.

She wasn't asking him to cure an incurable disease. All he had to do was join her at college. Most of the obstacles could be taken care of if he simply applied himself. Studying and…extra shifts at work might help with the finances. Student loans were a thing, too.

More than anything, he welcomed a challenge he could solve himself. Getting into college seemed way easier than dealing with shit he couldn't possibly fix.

As this ran through his mind, he reached the exit, and a beautiful voice called his name.

"Sakuta."

The aforementioned cutest girl was leaning against the 2-1 shoe lockers, waiting for him. Mai Sakurajima.

Glossy black hair, strong eyes, unblemished complexion. At five foot five, she was taller than many girls, and her slim build made her all the more striking. Even standing against these battered old

shoe lockers, she made everything around her look like a shot from a movie.

And that meant she always attracted attention. Perhaps this... presence was a by-product of experience—she'd been famous since she was very young. She'd taken a long hiatus but was back to work now, filming TV shows, movies, and commercials and modeling for fashion magazines. Her schedule was so busy she barely had time to go on dates with him.

Sakuta joined Mai and pulled off his slippers.

"Were you waiting for me?" he asked.

"*Someone* said they wanted to go home together 'every day.'"

He took his shoes out, replacing them with the slippers.

"Did I say that?"

"You did."

"I'm pretty sure what I said was 'Mai, you're graduating soon, so if you don't have work, we should make time for after-school *dates*.'"

He stressed that last word with a glance her way. She showed no sign of acknowledging it, swinging his shoe locker shut for him.

"Come on," she said, walking off before he even had his shoes on.

He hustled to catch up and was by her side before she reached the door. They headed toward the gate, the sun in their eyes.

Sakuta yawned.

"What, is walking with me boring you?"

Mai gave him a look. She had a smile on her lips, but not in her eyes. How dare he make her wait and then yawn in her face.

"I had a strange dream and still haven't fully woken up."

"Classes just ended, so sleep should not be part of the equation."

She rolled her eyes at him.

"Well, I always did hate English."

"You really should pay attention. Or do you not want to go to college with me?"

"Wait. I thought it was *you* who wanted to go to college with *me*."

"Yes, because *I'm* the one who loves *you*."

She didn't even turn to look at him.

But his heart had skipped a beat, and he'd swung toward her—so he lost this round. And when she did turn toward him, there was a challenge in her eyes. This was clearly a test to see if he'd just let that stand.

"I *do* want to go to college with you, Mai."

If Mai had a request, he was going to do his best to fulfill it. Especially if it was something he wanted himself. They'd promised to be happy together, and he felt like this was how to make that come true.

Outside the gate, the railroad crossing lay ahead. The warning bells were ringing, the railings coming down.

"Which way?" Mai asked.

She didn't specify. But he knew what she was asking. Anyone commuting to *this* school would only be wondering one thing here—which way was the train going?

"Fujisawa bound," he said.

To the right of the crossing was Shichirigahama Station. But there was no train waiting at the platform. To the left, a train came slowly rolling in from Kamakura, leaving Sakuta, Mai, and several other students stuck at the crossing.

The bells stopped, and the railings went up.

Several students took off, running pell-mell toward the station. They might manage to catch the train.

"Shall we?" Mai asked. If they missed this train, it was a twenty-minute wait for the next one. "Are you in a rush to get home?"

There was a hint of mischief in her eyes.

"When I'm with you, Mai, I always wish this barrier would stay down forever."

"That would get old fast."

They started moving, the last of the crowd to step into the crossing. Normal walking speed—missing this train just meant their after-school date would be twenty minutes longer. No point rushing.

Ahead of them lay a gentle downward slope. At the end of it, the Shichirigahama beach. When Sakuta took a deep breath, he could smell the salt on the breeze.

Even with the sea stretching out before them, they turned right after the crossing. On the other side of a little bridge, they spied the green sign above the station entrance.

Up a short staircase, they ran their train passes through the gates. The Fujisawa-bound train had just left, and only a dozen students remained. Most of them likely waiting for a Kamakura-bound train.

This station only had one set of tracks that led to a single platform. Trains came down those tracks from right and left, stopping at this platform. Their destinations alternated between Fujisawa and Kamakura. A single-line station with a touch of class.

There were no major thoroughfares or bustling shopping areas nearby, so it had a particular stillness to it, and time seemed to flow here at a more relaxed pace.

It only really got busy before and after school.

Depending on the season, if he accidentally overslept and arrived late, he'd often find himself the lone person disembarking here.

A train came in from Fujisawa, brakes screeching as it ground to a halt. Sakuta and Mai were waiting for a train bound the other direction.

Once passengers were loaded in, the green-and-cream retro-styled cars rolled slowly on out.

Sakuta and Mai included, there were maybe six or seven people left behind.

The wind carried in the clatter of the crossing bells, and then without warning, Mai reached out and took his hand. Well, finger—she was just lightly holding on to his pinkie. Her manager had warned them to be conscious of who was looking. This was probably a nod to that, a gesture in the direction of restraint.

And when he turned toward her, Mai didn't meet his eye. She just stared ahead at the tracks, saying nothing.

So he said nothing, either. Just admired her profile.

His heart satiated just by having her here with him.

Just feeling her warmth next to his…

…made him happy.

Nothing special. Just a normal afternoon. Headed home with Mai. A quiet time, watching the train roll out and waiting for the next one to arrive.

Not talking about anything in particular.

But Sakuta knew that these nothing moments were more precious than anything. That's why he couldn't take his eyes off Mai, watching her bask in the breeze. He could watch her forever, without ever getting bored. Each moment was a priceless treasure.

"What? You're staring."

Catching his gaze, she held her hair back against the wind, looking his way at last. She sounded tickled pink.

"Just making sure you're still here."

"Why wouldn't I be?" She spoke like she didn't get it, but her eyes said otherwise. "I know you went through a lot," she added. Slowly, like she was feeling it out. There was tenderness in her eyes.

"A bit too much, really."

Too much to ever put in words. He'd cried and cried, screamed his lungs out, grieved till his heart tore apart, and run until his legs could move no more. And smiled every bit as much.

It was precisely because he'd been through so much that he could fully appreciate moments like these. Just waiting for a train was now a source of joy—because they were here together. And because they shared that feeling.

"……"

"……"

They gazed into each other's eyes, neither looking away. Sakuta could feel his love for her welling up inside. The impulse taking hold.

"Um, Mai."

"Nooope," she said, like she was training a puppy. She tore her eyes away, seeming slightly embarrassed.

"I didn't even say anything yet."

"But you were about to suggest a kiss."

She glanced his way, making sure.

"But I *really* wanna."

Mai glanced around. There were more people on the platform now.

"You'll have to control yourself," she said. "I am."

She was keeping her voice low, so no one could hear.

Her hand had been wrapped around his pinkie this whole time, but she adjusted her grip, adding his ring finger. She squeezed it tight.

"Aww," he said in protest. That was hardly enough. But his desperate plea was brushed aside.

"Train's coming," she said.

Once they were aboard, the train carried them out of Shichirigahama Station along the coast. To the left of the car, outside the windows, they had a view of the ocean and Enoshima beyond.

There were plenty of tourists on board, glued to the view. Including some international visitors, who were snapping pictures like crazy. A common sight here.

Sakuta put Mai by the doorframe and held on to the strap above, watching the view go by. Well, watching Mai watch the view.

They stopped at Kamakura High School and Koshigoe, and then the train reached Enoshima Station. Loads of people got off, and half as many got back on. The waves of visitors headed out to Enoshima and coming back.

As the train pulled out again, Mai asked, "So what was this dream?"

"Mm?"

"The weird dream you had instead of English class."

"You were in it. Wearing a kid's backpack."

This was true, but it completely wiped the smile from her face.

"......"

It was replaced with a look of purest disgust. That was pleasant in its own right, but he concluded that he'd provoked an undeserved misapprehension, and he hastened to clarify.

"To be clear, I was not picturing the current *you* wearing that."

"Then what?" Her gaze was not getting warmer.

"You were maybe six years old."

"Hmph." She seemed taken aback. "That is weird."

"That's what I said."

"I thought you liked *older* women."

That wasn't what he'd meant, but if she'd latched on to that, he wasn't gonna argue the point.

"But this dream…" She lowered her voice, looking up at him. Intentionally. "It wasn't Adolescence Syndrome, was it?"

She sounded a little worried.

This was a mysterious phenomenon whispered about in corners of the Internet, a collective term for stories about the eyebrow-raising supernatural——spanning everything from reading minds to dreaming about the future.

"……"

And that grim look in her eyes was because they knew only too well those stories were not just idle online gossip.

Mai's own case of Adolescence Syndrome was actually what had brought them together in the first place.

"I think we're safe."

"Sakuta, sometimes it feels like Adolescence Syndrome is in love with you."

"And I'm grateful! It brought you to me."

"……"

She seemed unconvinced.

"I'm only dreaming of you 'cause you won't let me do anything. That must be why I'm seeing such strange things in my sleep."

He was definitely angling for attention.

And he soon got a poke on the cheek for it.

"Nice try," she said, digging her nail in.

"No matter what happens, Mai, I've got you. So I'll be okay."

"Always have something to say, don't you?"

She looked awfully pleased to be tormenting him again.

Fifteen minutes after leaving Shichirigahama, the train reached the end of the line—Fujisawa Station.

Outside the gates, Sakuta and Mai found themselves surrounded by department stores. This was a major city hub; the Enoden was not the only train line running through here. It also hosted the JR and Oda-kyu Enoshima Lines.

At this hour, the area was filled with local shoppers and students, all on their way home. They took the bridge over the bus terminal to the opposite side of the station. They both lived a ten-minute walk to the north.

"Need any groceries?" Mai asked as they passed the electronics store.

"Much as I'd love a supermarket date, I just bought some yesterday."

"Another day, then."

On their way, they crossed a bridge over the Sakai River. The farther they went from the station, the quieter things got. They were deep into a residential area now.

As they reached the park near their homes, Mai asked, "How's Kaede finding school?"

"She's all fired up and heading there every morning."

Sakuta's sister had been out of school for a long time, but toward the end of last year and over winter vacation, she'd done a lot of practice being outside. Her ultimate goal was to attend school in the new year, for third term. And at the moment, everything was going smoothly.

But she was still quite scared of her classmates' stares, so she was coming in a little late and spending the day studying in the nurse's office. She also staggered the time she left, returning home alone.

She still had a ways to go, which was exactly why she was all fired up.

Considering she'd spent a year and a half unable to leave the house at all, her achievements over the last month were incredibly impressive.

"I hope school gets easier for her."

"It will in time."

As they spoke, they reached their buildings. Mai lived in the one across from Sakuta, so their commutes matched perfectly.

"Oh, isn't that Kaede?"

Speak of the devil. Mai was looking down the road away from the station at a girl plodding their way. Mai was right—it was his sister.

She had a coat on over her junior high uniform. Her head was down, staring at the ground below her feet.

But then she looked up—perhaps feeling their eyes on her. She jumped, then recognized Sakuta and Mai and managed an awkward smile. Probably just normal awkwardness at running into friends outside.

She sped up a bit, coming over to them.

"Hi there, Kaede," Mai said.

"H-hi, Mai."

"You're wearing the coat!"

"Oh, yes! I love it."

She grinned bashfully. The coat was one Mai had passed on to her. Kaede was tall for her age, if not as tall as Mai; the coat had proved to be a good fit.

"You just got back?" she asked, turning to Sakuta, her tone abruptly turning sullen.

"As you can see."

"Hmm."

Her eyes glanced down at his hand. Mai was still holding on to him. Realizing this, she let go.

"Right, Sakuta, um…," Kaede began, but then trailed off.

"What?"

"Do you have plans for the next two days?"

That was evasive. He wasn't sure what she was asking.

"I plan to enjoy the heck out of the weekend," he said, equally nonspecific.

"So nothing," Kaede said, puffing up her cheeks.

He reached out and flattened them for her.

"Got a shift tomorrow."

"Sunday?"

"I'll be busy having a date with Mai, cuddling with Mai, and hopefully making out with Mai."

"Hngg."

Kaede made a grumpy noise.

"That sucks," she muttered, head down.

"Don't worry, Kaede. *I* have other plans."

"Aww. Work?" Sakuta's turn to be grumpy.

"Basically." Mai smiled, looking him right in the eye.

That rang false to him. If she had work, she was usually more specific. It felt like she was hiding something.

He was curious, but she didn't give him time to pry. Before he could ask, a white minivan pulled up, stopping next to them.

It was the same kind that Mai's manager drove. The driver was a woman in her midtwenties wearing a suit. Definitely Mai's manager—Ryouko Hanawa.

She got out, looking half mad, half at a loss. "You walked home together again?" she asked.

"We're a couple," Mai said. "It would be weird if we didn't."

"If someone snaps a picture and it turns into a whole thing..." Ryouko was sticking to her guns on this.

"That only happens when people try to hide it. Lies and denials fan the flames. I openly admitted I have a boyfriend, so there won't be any major uproar now."

Mai turned away like she was done listening. Ryouko was a few years older, and that seemed to bring out Mai's childish side.

"Listen, Mai…I know you've heard it before, but…"

But before she could launch into full lecture mode—

"Fine. I'll be careful," Mai said. Her show of obedience felt hollow.

"Argh, you *say* that, but don't mean it." Ryouko wailed. She definitely wasn't the one in control.

"I've gotta go," Mai said, turning back to Sakuta. "You'd better actually listen to Kaede, okay? Kaede, see you later."

Ryouko bobbed her head, then closed the door. The engine had been left running, so they soon pulled away.

"So what about this weekend?" Sakuta said as he watched the van pull around the corner.

Kaede's eyes were locked on the license plate. She seemed rather cross.

"Nothing," she said, sulking again.

"Kaede."

"What?" Still grumpy.

"You got something against Mai?"

"O-of course not! She's nice and pretty and cool! I'd love to be like her!"

"Then I have some invaluable advice."

"What?"

"When we get home, look in the mirror."

"Don't need to. I already know I'll never be like her."

Kaede glared at him, her cheeks all puffed up. This was the opposite of intimidating.

"Then why are you so grumpy?"

"It's your fault."

She was only getting worse. Teenage sisters were hard work.

"Huh?" he said, at a total loss.

"You're totally obsessed with her."

"Well, yeah. Anyone with a girlfriend that cute would be."

"Oh, I get it. I just hate it."

She didn't even want to look at him. It was an obvious appeal for attention.

"Something happen at school?"

Kaede still hadn't said what was up.

"I had a talk with a teacher."

She must be talking about Miwako Tomobe, her school's counselor.

"And?"

"About future plans."

She shifted uncomfortably, looking up at him through her lashes.

"Ahhh, future plans, huh?"

"Yeah."

"Whose?"

"*Mine*, obviously."

"I thought so."

It wasn't like it he hadn't thought about it. Kaede was in her third year of junior high. And it was the third term. Not much time left before graduation. But she'd only been back at school for ten days. Any plans beyond that just didn't feel real to him.

But hearing it from her forced him to admit that it was way past time.

"The teacher said we should get in touch with Dad."

Kaede gave him a searching look. He knew what he had to do.

"Okay, I'll ask him."

"Mm. Thanks."

She looked a lot less tense now.

"Do you actually have any idea what you want to do yet?" he asked, checking their mailbox and opening the auto-lock door.

"Not really," she said, trailing after him. "It's all so sudden."

But when he met her eye, she quickly turned away.

Sakuta felt pretty sure she *did* have a high school in mind.

But wasn't ready to tell him.

"Fair," he said, acting like he hadn't noticed.

He pressed the button for the elevator.

2

Two days later, Sunday, January 18.

The intercom rang exactly at one PM, as promised.

Sakuta met Miwako Tomobe at the door and led her into the living room, where his father and Kaede were waiting.

"Hello, Kaede."

"Hi."

"Sorry to take time out of your Sunday," their father said, bowing.

"Not at all. I'm the one imposing on your weekend."

"Please sit."

He waved her to a chair, and she took a seat at the dining table. She'd started to hang her coat on the back of it, but Sakuta brought it over to the rack at the door. He'd cleaned up that morning, but Nasuno's hair just would *not* stay off winter clothing. Nasuno was their calico cat, currently observing events from on top of the *kotatsu*. Two strangers were in the house, and she was very curious.

When Sakuta finished up at the rack, he went right past the table to the kitchen, where he got a pot of tea ready.

While he was busy with that, Miwako was talking about Kaede's test results. Or rather, explaining why she was the point person on that—this was usually handled by the homeroom teacher, but since Kaede had been out of school for so long, someone had suggested it would be easier on her if the school counselor handled things. Miwako had taken that proposal to Kaede, and they'd decided it was probably the best plan.

Kaede was nodding.

Sakuta lined up four steaming cups on a tray, unpacked the dove-shaped *rakugan* candy their father had brought, and carried it all to the table.

"Here you go," he said, placing Miwako's share in front of her.

"Thanks. Oh, these look good," she said. "Do you mind?"

And with that, she popped a *rakugan* into her mouth and savored the taste.

Sakuta moved a chair to the head of the table and sat next to Kaede. She was looking rather tense. Back bolt upright, hands folded on her lap, not even looking up. Her eyes locked on the teacup he'd placed before her.

"Well, I'm sure you're aware, but I'm here today to discuss Kaede's future."

"Right."

Their father nodded quietly. He had come wearing the same suit he wore to work. The jacket was off, but the necktie was crisp.

When he'd arrived at their door half an hour earlier, Sakuta had thought he was being really uptight, but now he realized it was totally the right choice.

Especially with Miwako seated opposite, in full business wear, jacket and all.

"She's only just returned to school, so ideally, we wouldn't be having this conversation until she's fully adjusted, but the deadline for most high school exam applications is at the end of January. That's why I suggested we meet to discuss it."

She took a thick A4-size folder out of her bag, pulled several documents out of it, and put them on the table.

"This exam schedule is mostly prefecture-run high schools. Applications must be turned in between January twenty-eighth and the thirtieth. The exams themselves are on February sixteenth, with interviews taking place over a three-day period from the sixteenth to the eighteenth. Results are announced on February twenty-seventh. Private schools might be a week earlier, and many have already begun."

"Um," their father said when she paused for breath.

"Yes? Anything unclear?"

"No, er…"

Their father hesitated, eyes turning to Kaede. Clearly, this was something hard to say. Trying to refocus, he said, "Excuse me," and had a sip of tea. Once he'd swallowed, he turned back to Miwako and took a deep breath.

"Will Kaede actually be ready for high school?"

His meaning was clear, and Kaede's shoulders twitched. That question got right to the heart of the matter and was definitely crucial. That's why he said it out loud, even though it was hard to do with her here. No hemming and hawing, no beating around the bush.

"I'm sure everybody knows, but just so we're clear—junior high is part of the mandatory education system, so regardless of attendance, she *will* graduate in March."

"Right."

"As far as attending high school goes, Kaede's academic abilities are certainly one concern," Miwako said, pulling another page out of her thick folder.

This was a graded answer sheet. With *Kaede Azusagawa* at the top.

"This is a copy of last year's prefectural entrance exam. I had Kaede take it last Friday."

Having her test results on display made Kaede go even stiffer. A brief scan of the marks showed it was an even split between right and wrong.

"The minimal cutoff will certainly limit her prospects, but if she can replicate this performance, not only are there schools that will take her, but she'll have a selection available."

Kaede had said she understood a solid portion of junior high material despite having no memory of learning it. Her dissociative disorder had left her with amnesia, and the other Kaede had spent two years studying for her. It was proof that the other Kaede had existed. Every right answer on this sheet was a gift from her. That realization put a heat behind his eyes, a sting in his nose. Sakuta took a loud sip of tea to hide it.

Kaede glanced at him in surprise. Their eyes met, and she quickly looked away. He was about to ask why, but Miwako and his father were talking again, and he didn't want to interrupt.

"But with prefectural schools, aren't her grades a major factor?"

"They are," Miwako said, nodding. "The exact ratio varies by school, but the transcript is usually forty to fifty percent of the evaluation. The interview is twenty percent. That means the exam itself is only thirty to forty percent of the decision."

"The exams are less important than I imagined, then."

Sakuta felt like he really hadn't understood the system when it was his turn. All he'd really cared about was going somewhere far away.

"The interview and exam count for more than they did when we were still using the standardized achievement test. I was the last generation to go through that, but in my day, it was fifty percent grades and twenty percent achievement test results, so before you even took the exam, seventy percent of your fate was decided. Although in my case, that meant the exam itself was stress-free."

Sakuta vaguely remembered a junior high teacher mentioning that Kanagawa had previously had a unique system involving a test like that. It had been abandoned a while back, resulting in the current approach.

"I took that myself," their father said.

Sakuta had never stopped to wonder, but of course their father had gone to high school in Kanagawa. A new nugget of knowledge.

Next to him, Kaede still had her head down, not joining in. Her hands were clenched. Did she have something on her mind?

Since she wasn't talking, Sakuta spoke up.

"But all that makes it sound like prefecture admissions are stacked against her."

And that left them with private schools. Which were much more expensive and thus a point of concern for him.

"Yes, the prefecture admissions system places Kaede at a distinct disadvantage."

Since she had never attended classes, she essentially had *no* grades. And given her personality, she was unlikely to impress in an interview. Miwako was phrasing it gently, but to his ears, it didn't sound remotely realistic.

"And in cases like that, we recommend private schools that offer open enrollment."

"That offer what?"

He'd never heard that term before, and he looked to Miwako for explanation.

But his father answered first.

"In this case, I assume you mean schools that accept students based purely on the entrance exam results?"

"That's correct," Miwako replied. "Those tests also tend to be administered later in the season. We would still have a lot of work to do, but it would also give us a little more time to prepare."

Listening to Miwako, Sakuta studied his father's reaction. He sure seemed to know a lot about this subject. Sakuta had only started looking into it the day before and was feeling totally outclassed. His father had prepped for this. And that meant he'd been thinking about Kaede's future for a while, aware that this day might come.

"But regardless of the admissions policy, private schools do tend to be much more expensive."

Miwako pulled out another document and placed it before their father. A standard listing of entrance fees and three-year tuitions.

It was an eye-popping figure. Certainly not something a high schooler's part-time job could cover.

"And these documents are for schools that Kaede's academic abilities would permit."

She laid out five or six pamphlets.

"I've limited it to schools within easy commuting distance of this address, but if we broaden that range a bit, there are other choices. At any rate, on the academic performance front, Kaede does have options for advancement."

"Okay."

Stage one cleared. But neither grown-up was looking any less stern. Clearly, the next stage was the real issue. Sakuta knew that himself, and judging by Kaede's pursed lips, she did, too.

"Having said all that, from the perspective of a school counselor, it's difficult for me to recommend that Kaede attend a conventional high school."

She was clearly choosing her words carefully, keeping one eye on Kaede's reactions the whole time.

"It's unfortunately quite common for students who struggle to attend junior high to run into the same issues in high school."

"Yes," their father said, encouraging her to continue.

"High schools can force students to repeat a year, which can marginalize them even more. I've seen any number of students drop out as a result."

Miwako's eyes drifted to the table, her expression ambivalent. Some of those students had likely been in her care. It made sense that she felt responsible for their outcomes and regretted her inability to help them.

"If junior high doesn't go well, and high school is the same...it's difficult to regain confidence. And that can have a huge toll on later stages in life. Certainly, it doesn't turn out that way for everybody, but it is a strong possibility."

There was no way to know what would happen. Maybe Kaede would start high school, make some good friends, and enjoy herself. Maybe she'd come home every day full of stories about the good times she'd had.

But if someone pointed out that possibility was highly unlikely, Sakuta couldn't argue with that.

He was more inclined to wonder what Kaede should do instead.

"As far as nonconventional options go, we have these."

Miwako took another A4-size folder out of her bag. Also really thick. More high school brochures emerged, spread out on the table for them to see.

At first glance, they looked standard enough—but every school name was followed by the words *remote learning*.

Neither his father nor Kaede reacted to this. They knew. This wasn't news for them. Miwako must have mentioned it to Kaede before. And their father had likely done his homework here, too.

"Each school handles things differently, but largely you're watching prerecorded lectures and studying at home, at your own pace. You regularly submit assignments to earn the credits needed to graduate. This system avoids the issue of being unable to fit in, and the graduation accreditation received is no different from an ordinary high school."

Sakuta picked up a pamphlet and flipped through it. He couldn't really get a feel for what kind of school it was, but they had photographs of normal-looking field trips, school festivals, and classrooms. None of that seemed any different from the schools he knew.

The students were all smiling. They looked to be having a lot more fun than Sakuta, who spent his days in the periphery of his class.

"Kaede has only just started attending school again, so I would suggest taking the next three years to slowly readjust."

"I've heard remote-learning students are less likely to last until graduation or advance to higher education afterward."

"That's unfortunately true. These schools are certainly not without their flaws. Since you're not going in every day, you have to be responsible for you own progress, and that means family support is all the more vital."

"……"

Their father nodded grimly. He was clearly unsure what would be best for Kaede. He knew Miwako was speaking from experience, and that carried weight. But Sakuta also knew why his father was uncertain. Both of them were thinking of Kaede's future.

So he left the fretting to the adults and turned to his sister.

"What do *you* want to do?" he asked.

She jumped and slowly raised her head. She gave Sakuta a long look, sensed eyes on her, and glanced toward the adults. Then she hung her head again.

Just sitting there while everyone talked about you was enough to wear anyone out. And for a girl like Kaede, it would take a physical toll as well. But this had to be Kaede's decision. It was her life.

"I...," she began, then cut herself off.

Nobody rushed her. They just waited for her to speak again. At her own pace.

Maybe Nasuno was worried. She came over and hopped up onto Kaede's lap. Kaede gently petted her for a moment. Maybe that helped settle her down.

"I want...to be like everyone else," she said softly.

Miwako reacted first. Brow furrowing, slightly lost.

Sakuta wasn't sure how she felt, but verbally...she neither agreed nor disagreed.

"You mean you'd prefer a conventional high school?" she asked, quietly confirming what Kaede really wanted.

Kaede simply nodded. Twice, for emphasis.

"Anywhere specific?"

Her hand stopped stroking Nasuno. That convinced Sakuta she *did* have a school in mind.

"Well...," she whispered, her voice barely audible. No further words emerged.

"Talking's free," Sakuta said. This seemed like it could take a while, so he popped a dove-shaped *rakugan* into his mouth. It felt like it absorbed all the moisture there, but that made the tea taste really good.

When he put his cup back down, he could tell Kaede wanted to speak. There were a lot of emotions in her eyes as she glanced up at him. He figured it out. It was obvious which school she was thinking about now. The fact that she was staring at him was the answer.

"Kaede, if you want some, help yourself," he said, acting like he didn't get it precisely because he did.

"That's not it," she groused, frustrated.

"Oh, tea? I'll get you another cup."

Miwako's cup was empty, too, so he got to his feet, pretending he was getting refills. Mai would definitely have been stifling a laugh at this. But neither grown-up present said anything. And Sakuta didn't actually move toward the kitchen. Before he could...

"Where Sakuta goes," Kaede managed. Barely audible.

Not looking up, she spoke again a bit louder. "I want to go to Sakuta's high school."

She'd gotten her feelings out in the open.

Miwako looked extra lost. She'd just finished explaining the challenge prefectural schools entailed. And Minegahara's admission standards were on the high side. Third from the top in this area. Kaede likely stood no chance of getting in, and her face made it clear she was well aware of that.

"Okay," their father said. He took her words at face value without hesitation.

Sakuta put his hand on her head.

"You should've said so in the first place," he said, grinning her fears away.

Ultimately, they decided not to make up their minds that day. They spoke a while longer, and then Miwako took her leave.

From her professional standpoint, she couldn't offer false hopes.

"You can apply to Minegahara High, but your chances of getting in are almost nonexistent," she said. There was no getting around it.

The reasons were exactly what Sakuta suspected. Forty percent of the admission standards depended on her transcript, and twenty on the interview. And most applicants would be able to score higher on the exam than Kaede could now. She could try to study for it, but the exam was only a month away.

Three factors, none of which Kaede could really do much about. "Almost nonexistent" essentially meant "definitely not."

And after laying those harsh truths out, Miwako added, "I'm against applying there at all. Time is limited, and we should be focused on a more realistic option. I want to get you ready for that."

A reasonable, mature opinion.

And that made Kaede go into her room, shut the door, and not come out, which effectively ended the meeting.

"I'm the bad guy here, aren't I?" Miwako said, looking dejected.

"She'll forget it once she's had some pudding," Sakuta assured her as they said their good-byes.

After taking the elevator back to their floor, he saw his father was at the door, getting ready to leave.

"Going already?"

"Yeah."

Almost curt. Sakuta didn't have to ask why he was in a rush. His father not giving a reason explained it all.

He was worried about their mother.

"Kaede is…?"

"Still in her room. I said I was leaving, and she just said, 'Okay.'"

"Lovely."

He followed their father out. They rode the elevator down together. Neither spoke.

When they got to the street, Sakuta said "Bye" and raised a hand.

"Sakuta."

"Mm?"

He turned back.

"What do *you* want to do?"

After all that talk about Kaede's future, his father had finally asked about his.

"College," he said, not even thinking or worrying about it. Kaede had voiced her desires, so he had to do the same. "I'll cover what I can myself, but it won't be enough, so…I'll need help."

Figured it couldn't hurt to ask. He'd never really put on a serious face and begged for help before, and it was a little nerve-racking.

"Okay," his father said. He looked almost happy. It felt like a long time since Sakuta had seen him smile.

"That something worth grinning about?" he asked.

But his father didn't answer. "Look after Kaede," he said instead.

He headed toward the station. Walking quickly. He was soon out of sight.

Sakuta watched him go, feeling like maybe he understood that smile after all.

He had been happy.

To be asked. To be relied upon.

3

Monday morning.

Homeroom ended, and Sakuta left class, chasing after the teacher.

"Azusagawa? That's a new one. What?"

"You wanted me to turn in the survey, right?"

He held out a piece of paper. The teacher took it on reflex and glanced down, and his face froze.

Sakuta had put the name of two Yokohama area universities, one nationally run and one city run. The sheet layout had them as his first and second choice, but he didn't really have a preference.

But these choices *would* be a surprise.

"There you have it."

"We'll need to have a little chat."

He was frowning, but he didn't call him crazy yet. Probably because Sakuta had done well on the mock exam they'd taken in the middle of second term.

That was because Mai had helped him study. If he hadn't done well, she would've been livid, so he'd really given it his all. Humans could do wonders with sufficient motivation.

"I'll definitely need your advice," he said politely.

This seemed to surprise his teacher even more, but in a good way.

"All right," he said, looking proud.

Sakuta paid attention in class that morning, too. Math, physics, English, and math again. Everything but English was part of the elective science curriculum, and the students were 90 percent male. Not exactly a feast for the eyes.

After that dull gray morning ended and lunchtime arrived, Sakuta quickly fled the room, empty-handed.

Students racing to the bakery truck passed him. On the stairs, he passed upperclassmen racing down.

Going against the flow, Sakuta headed for the third floor.

At the very back of a long hall was an empty classroom. He opened the door and stepped in.

Nobody ever came here—except the girl waiting for him.

"Oh, Sakuta," Mai said, turning around.

She had two desks pushed together by the window, facing each other. There were two lunch box–size bags in her hands.

Mai had called him last night. "I'll make something, so let's eat lunch together."

He wasn't about to turn a lunch date down.

The window seats had a great view of the ocean. They sat down across from each other, and Mai opened up the lunches she'd made. Well-seasoned chicken nuggets. Rolled eggs with chopped *shiso* mixed in. Potato salad peppered with crispy bacon. And the rice was sprinkled with sesame, a pickled plum at the center. Each dish had an extra wrinkle to it, and they were all very good. Sakuta made a big show of enjoying it and managed to wheedle Mai into feeding him a single bite.

If they were together, just the act of eating lunch was a source of joy.

"That was great."

"It was nothing."

And that made the meal go quick.

"But what brought this on, Mai?" he asked while helping putting the empty lunch boxes away.

"Why is that a question?"

"No ulterior motives?"

His eyes were on the bags she'd carried them in.

"I just felt like cooking for you, Sakuta."

That was adorable.

Mai put the bags into her backpack and took out several thin B5-size booklets. The top cover had *Foreign Languages: English (Writing)* on it. There were further instructions below that, but Mai turned the page before he could read them. He thought he'd seen something about an answer sheet, though. This clearly involved test problems. And given the timing, it was likely related to the National Center Test for University Admissions.

"What's that, Mai?" he asked, pointing at it. His heart sinking.

Mai took out her phone and punched something into it, checking the book as she did.

"Problems for the Center Test."

His fears had come true.

"From previous years?"

"Nope, this year."

"This year?"

"Yep, this year."

She was busy with her phone and not looking at him.

"......"

"......"

"Um, why this year's Center Test?"

"Because I spent the last two days taking it."

Even now, she was going back and forth from the booklet to her phone. She finished up English and flipped to a book of math problems.

"So what are you doing, exactly?" he asked, pointing at her phone.

"Self-grading."

She made that sound obvious, but it sure didn't make sense to him.

"This makes it easy. You can just punch in your answers, and it'll calculate your results for you."

She must have gotten through all subjects, because she showed

Sakuta the final score. He wasn't clear on the detailed breakdown, but out of 900 possible points, she'd earned 830. The smile on her face made it extremely clear that this was a very good number. Less than 10 percent wrong, and that alone was really impressive. She probably had a perfect score on several subjects.

"You took it this year, though?"

"Yes."

"What happened to taking a year off and enjoying campus life with yours truly?"

"I'm taking the test this year, then a year's leave of absence."

"Because?"

"I figured that would make you hit the books like a madman."

She had her face cupped in both hands and wore a look of absolute delight. The effervescent smile from her sports drink commercials. The one he'd heard a boy from another school deem "too cute for words" on the train to school that morning. And it was all for him. That itself was pure bliss, but Sakuta couldn't quite stop to savor it.

This was the real reason why she'd summoned him to lunch.

The homemade meal had drawn him in so she could drive the hammer home better.

If they'd taken the tests together and he slipped up and didn't make the cut, he could have hoped she'd opt to console him—but she'd mercilessly cut off that escape route with a smile.

A bad idea crossed his mind. National university admissions had two stages. She still had that second round ahead of her. If he could make her blow that...

"You're gonna try and make me fail?"

"I would never..."

She'd read his mind. Sakuta looked out the window, trying to collect himself. He basked in the vastness of the sea for a moment, then turned back to her.

"I was just wondering what reward I'd get for applying myself."

He'd do what he could. Had always meant to. He had the motivation.

But the thought of studying for days on end was still deeply depressing. He needed a light in that darkness.

"Then let's make it a date," Mai said, like the idea had just hit her. "I don't have work today, so we can go after school. They've got tulips on Enoshima, I hear."

She showed him a photo of them on her phone.

He would normally jump on that, but it wasn't an option today.

"Ohhh," he said, shifting guiltily.

"What? You don't wanna?" Mai's eyes narrowed.

"I have a thing…"

"Work?"

"Basically," he said evasively.

"Payback for Friday?" There was a gleam in Mai's eyes that definitely went beyond "disappointed."

"Absolutely not. I would never hide anything from you, Mai."

"So you definitely are."

She fixed him with her most merciless glare but didn't maintain it long.

"Okay, fine. If you're brushing me off, it's *definitely* about Kaede."

Mai knew Kaede had been trying to say something on Friday, so it was easy for her to make that leap.

"Basically."

"Hmm? Well, okay, then."

She still seemed pretty disgruntled. She was grinding his foot beneath the desk. But she'd taken her slipper off, so it didn't actually hurt. It was honestly rather pleasant—and that must have shown on his face, because she pressed harder.

"Um, Mai…"

"Yes?" she said, all innocence.

"Never mind."

He decided to let her stomp away. That was what he got for turning down a date from his adorable girlfriend. Sakuta wanted to be the kind of man who could take a little spite, so this worked out great. A prime opportunity to become a better person.

4

After school, Sakuta was on cleaning duty. Once the class was swept, he headed for the faculty office—a place he usually did his best to avoid.

His teacher had stopped him right after the final homeroom.

"Azusagawa, swing by the office."

"Does that mean I don't have to clean?"

"Do that first, but make sure you come see me after."

He was firm enough that Sakuta knew he couldn't get away with pretending to forget. Wondering what this was about, he opened the door and bowed to everyone inside.

He looked around the faculty office. It was as big as two classrooms. His homeroom teacher was sitting near the center, and when their eyes met, he got up and came over, carrying several printouts.

"Fill these out and let's see where you are."

The top page had *Foreign Languages: English (Writing)* at the top. He'd seen that before. And there were a bunch of rules for taking the test below it.

Clearly a copy of the Center Test problem books—the same test Mai had been self-grading at lunch.

When Sakuta just stared at them, the teacher pushed them into his hands.

"Five subjects, and your target score is 750 out of 900."

"That's fast. I just handed in my survey today."

"You're already behind. Everyone else started last summer."

Sakuta had meant his teacher's turnaround, but the man smoothly flipped it on him. Arguably a positive spin.

"Huh…"

"You said you wanted advice, right?" The teacher scowled at him. "Get those done."

"Got it."

The teachers had a meeting or something, and he was soon called away, allowing Sakuta to make his getaway.

"Thanks," he said, but no one was listening. He closed the door behind him.

As he walked away, he stuffed the pages in his bag. Free at last.

Between cleaning and the summons, he was a solid half hour behind his usual schedule. The school felt much quieter than it did when he typically left.

Anyone headed home was long since gone. By now, only students with clubs or practice were still around. The halls themselves were empty. He could hear some sports team or other yelling out on the field, but from this distance, it all felt like a lazy afternoon. Sakuta reached the exit without spotting another soul.

He'd figured Mai wouldn't wait for him.

But he'd sort of hoped she would.

She sometimes hung around like that, just to surprise him.

And that would have been a comfort today.

Sadly, she wasn't leaning against his shoe locker today.

There was nobody here at all.

He'd been forced to turn down their after-school date, and this was the harsh reality.

"I *did* see it coming…," he grumbled.

He opened his shoe locker—and a folded scrap of paper fluttered out. "Mm?"

Blinking, he scooped it up.

It said *Twit* in Mai's handwriting.

She was clearly still holding the date refusal against him. But if she was making the first move, she probably wasn't that mad. This felt more like a ploy to ensure he indulged her later.

Amused by that, he started grinning.

Then he noticed another note in much smaller letters.

Wipe that grin off your face.

She really knew him well.

And that just made him grin harder.

Moments like these were the absolute best.

Sakuta's grin lasted all through his shoe change and the walk to the station. He carefully tucked the note into his uniform pocket.

At the station, Sakuta hopped on a train at Shichirigahama and watched the sea roll by on the way to Fujisawa Station.

The clock on the Enoden Fujisawa platform said four thirty.

He went through the gates and through the crowds on the overpass. Past the JR and Odakyu gates and out the north exit.

His way home led down the road past the electronics store, but today he turned the other direction.

Sakuta worked at a family restaurant near the station. The sun was getting pretty low, so the view inside those windows was glowing extra bright.

Outside the shop, he found a familiar face.

A tall boy with a jacket over his server's uniform. One of Sakuta's few friends, Yuuma Kunimi. He had a broom in hand and was sweeping the area.

"Kunimi," he called.

Yuuma looked up and saw him. "Mm, Sakuta? You have a shift today?"

"I thought *you* had practice."

Yuuma was on the basketball team. Any time they had an exhibition match in the gym, the place filled up with shrieking girls—he was *very* popular.

"Got an away game Saturday, so we're off today."

"Then you should rest up, man."

Working a shift undermined the whole point of skipping practice.

"Everyone's out doing *something*. Work's no different."

He spoke truth with a breezy smile.

"So why you here?"

"Meeting someone."

"Sakurajima?"

"Nope."

"Don't have *too* many affairs."

"I ain't as popular as you, so no danger of that."

Sakuta peered through the window. The clock said 4:40. He still had twenty minutes to go, and inside he'd just sit there bored, so he figured he might as well keep distracting Yuuma.

"Kunimi."

"Mm?"

A leaf came fluttering in from somewhere, and Yuuma swept it into the dustpan.

"You got plans for after high school?"

"Where'd that come from?" Yuuma laughed, like the question was totally out of character.

"Isn't it on all our minds? We're doing those survey things."

"Fair enough. But you're going to college, right? With Sakurajima?"

"Did I tell you that?"

He couldn't recall doing anything of the sort.

"Futaba told me."

Yuuma's source was a mutual friend of theirs. Rio Futaba, a girl in their year. She filled her afternoons with science club experiments and was probably glasses deep in one now. Or kicking back with some instant coffee she'd brewed in a beaker over a Bunsen burner.

"She said, 'Azusagawa's *really* looking forward to it.'"

"Is it just me, or does that sound like an insult more than anything else?"

"I think most people would just call it jealousy. Which I get!"

"But you've got a firecracker of your own."

"Kamisato's only like that with you. You fight with her again? She was mega-pissed at you on Friday."

"Don't worry. I already forgot it."

"So it was definitely your fault." Yuuma laughed out loud.

He'd likely heard the whole story. Saki Kamisato had been forced to read aloud after Sakuta drifted off in class, so he hadn't actively *done* anything, but the blame did almost certainly lie on his shoulders.

"But that's cool. College sounds like fun."

Yuuma put his chin on the broom handle. Eyes on the sky above.

"I don't wanna study like that, though," he joked.

"You get to skip all that, Kunimi. You're a lucky man."

"Nah, I gotta do a bit."

"For what?"

"Employment exam."

"For what?"

"Firefighter."

"Huh."

First he'd heard of it, but it made perfect sense somehow. Sakuta could only use his own yardstick here, but it felt like a very Yuuma choice. The kind of job he wanted dedicated men like Yuuma doing.

"Well, if our place ever goes up, I'm counting on you."

"Fire safety starts at home."

They were both laughing now.

"You tell Futaba that?"

"It's what she told *me*."

"Her diabolical plan to put you out of work. Revenge for turning her down, huh? Well done, Futaba."

"If we could end all fires and disasters, I'd happily get another job. Not that I have this one yet."

Yuuma grinned happily. He totally wasn't joking at all, one of the things Sakuta liked most about him.

"Well, when you get your first paycheck, we'll have to celebrate. Get me and Futaba something good."

"If *you're* paying."

They were still laughing when a voice called his name.

He turned around and saw Miwako Tomobe standing there. Ten minutes early.

"You really do like older women," Yuuma muttered, but Sakuta pretended not to hear.

5

He sat in a booth with Miwako, talking for the better part of an hour.

By the time he paid and left, it was night. The sky above was growing dark. The lights around were all aglow.

He walked Miwako to the JR gates.

"Thanks for taking the time today," he said, bowing his head.

"Let me know if anything comes up," she said with a wave—and was off down the platform.

Alone, he left the station and trudged down the road home. This took a good ten minutes. He reached his apartment building and looked up at the building across the street. Mai's condo was the corner room on the ninth floor.

The windows were dark.

Maybe she'd gone to bed early, still mad at him for blowing off that date idea. He'd have to call her later and get back on her good side.

With that thought in mind, he took the elevator to the fifth floor.

He took out his keys and opened the door to their apartment.

He stepped inside and found less room at his feet than expected. There were more shoes than usual. Those weren't Sakuta's or Kaede's. Two extra pairs, neither of which he recognized.

He could hear girls' voices in the living room. They must have company.

"I'm back!" he called, taking his shoes off.

He poked his head around the corner, and a voice called from the kitchen.

"Welcome home, Sakuta."

Mai was there, in an apron, peeling potatoes.

"We've occupied your kitchen," she said.

"Any particular reason?"

"I bumped into Kaede on my way home. Sakuta, you didn't tell Kaede you'd be home late, did you?"

He suspected that wasn't entirely true.

Odds were, she'd planned to cook for Kaede precisely because she'd known he had a thing and wouldn't be home.

That certainly explained Mai's presence. And if he got to see her in an apron and eat dinner with her, well, what could be better? He'd happily watch her cook for the rest of his life.

But there was a second guest. A blond high school girl sitting at the dining table. Her uniform didn't match the boldly dyed hair at all—it was a prim and proper girls' school uniform, one of those places where the history was storied. This was Nodoka Toyohama, Mai's sister from another mother and a member of the idol group Sweet Bullet.

"Oh, 'sup," she said, barely glancing his way. She soon turned back to Kaede, who was sitting opposite her and listening intently. His sister had a notebook open in front of her and was scribbling furiously.

He looked closer and saw an English textbook open between them. Nodoka was reading the lines aloud, tracing along with her finger—and her accent was shockingly good. And not only that, she was translating into Japanese on the fly and explaining the reasoning to Kaede. "So the *on* here is…"

Her flashy makeup and dyed hair sure didn't make her look like the kind of girl who could study, but that uniform was from one of the toughest schools to get into in all Yokohama. She shattered stereotypes.

"Why are you here, Toyohama?"

"My sister said she was cooking at your place, so I came with."

"Well, don't. It's time you learned to fend for yourself."

Nodoka had washed up in Mai's place last fall, and they were living together now. Having her permanently there was definitely cramping Sakuta's style. Kaede was always at his place, so it was a real challenge finding anywhere for the two of them to relax together.

"Gonna take at least five more years."

A very specific number.

"Five?! Gimme a break here!"

Clearly too long.

"I mean, going to college from her place is closer than from home, so…"

Even worse, Nodoka insisted she *had* to attend the same university as Mai. The exact place Sakuta was trying to get into.

"Just promise you won't go for the same major."

They were the same age, so if they both applied to the same department, that would be one less slot available to him.

"Oh, but…no, wait."

An idea struck him.

"Same major might work, actually."

"Huh? You think you can get your scores in my league in *one* year?"

There was a challenge in that glare. She'd helped him study before, so she was *well* aware of his shortcomings. But book smarts didn't mean she could figure out what Sakuta was thinking. There were many things in this world not measurable by admissions standards.

"No, Nodoka. He's just going to blame you if he fails."

Mai, on the other hand, knew exactly what he was thinking.

"Right. Definitely picking a completely different department."

"Don't be like that, Doka! We can be in all the same classes! Live the campus life!"

This nickname was used by her fans and provoked a look of utter disgust.

He figured it would be best to stop teasing her for now.

Partly because Nodoka was nearing her boiling point, but mostly because Kaede had been stealing furtive glances at him since he came in.

He finally met her eye.

"Welcome back," she said. A bit late.

"Good to be home."

"……"

Kaede clearly wanted to say something, but she didn't. Mai came out of the kitchen and put her hands on Kaede's shoulders.

"You need to talk to Sakuta, right?" she asked, leaning over her shoulder.

Kaede nodded once, then got up. She stood right in front of him.

"I—I……!"

Her voice was very loud. Nasuno was in the corner, and the noise woke her up. Even the cat was listening.

"Er, um. I just…"

She got her volume under control, looking up at Sakuta.

"I still want to go to your school," she managed, her voice shaking a little. Eyes anxious and stressed. "That's what I want. I want to take the exams there."

Sakuta didn't glance away. He listened till she was done.

Her hands were clenched over her stomach. She was *still* fighting off her anxiety.

"Then fill this out," he said, like it was no big deal. He pulled a hefty A4-size envelope out of his bag and put it on top of Kaede's head.

"Wh-what is it?"

Confused, she reached for it. And pulled out a single sheet of rather thick paper.

Her eyes scanned it and found the words *Enrollment Application* at the top.

"Er…huh?! How…?"

"Ms. Tomobe gave it to me."

This was why he'd met with Miwako even if it meant spurning Mai's invitation. He'd planned to make a plea for letting Kaede apply to Minegahara, but Miwako was one step ahead of him. The second she sat down in the booth, she'd handed over the application. Apparently, she had already known why he'd called her there.

She let him know exactly how conflicted she was about it. It was a grown-up's job to make it clear what could and could not be done. At the same time, it was just as important to respect what her charges wanted.

She'd said that ultimately her responsibility was to give support while keeping one eye on what lay beyond. Which was why she'd given him the form.

"So hit them books."

"I will. But can I ask a favor?"

He could imagine where this was going. So he deliberately acted like he didn't. "Mm?"

Mai and Nodoka were giving him warm looks. It was super uncomfortable.

"Help me study," Kaede said, like she was expecting a no.

But he already had his answer ready.

"Don't blame me if you fail."

And with that, he headed into his room to change.

The door half-closed, he got his uniform off. Just as he hit undies only, he heard Mai and Nodoka cheering her on. Kaede had reached the starting line at last.

There was just one huge problem hanging overhead.

"Do I even remember junior high school stuff?"

Sakuta's own educational standards might yet prove his Achilles' heel.

Chapter
2

walking speed

1

The water in the beaker neared the boiling point, and bubbles started popping on the surface. At first, they were spread out, but they soon came faster and faster in a vaporous chorale.

Sakuta listened to the sounds as he scowled at the list of problems designed to help him prep for exams. Thinking about the answer to a question about the law of conservation of energy.

But as his frown deepened, someone interrupted his thought process.

"So…Azusagawa…"

"Mm?"

He looked up. One of his few friends was seated across the lab table—Rio Futaba.

Glasses signifying intellect, long hair bound at the back, short—only five foot one—and today she was once again wearing a white lab coat over her uniform.

"You said you were prepping for the same college as Sakurajima, right?"

Rio pulled the alcohol burner out from under the beaker and put the cap on, extinguishing the flame. She was talking to Sakuta but had not once looked his way. Keeping her attention firmly on the fire she wielded. Her vow to destroy Yuuma Kunimi's future firefighting career was alive and well.

"Yep, like I said. Studying's gonna be a nightmare."

Mai just *had* to specify a national university. Which required all five Center Test subjects. Which meant he had that much more prep ahead of him.

Figuring it was best to figure out where he stood, he went through the problems from the Center Test Mai had taken that year—and the results were not promising.

Sakuta had only managed 505 out of a combined 900 total. Only 55 percent of his answers were right.

If this were a school test, that wouldn't technically be a failing grade, but the Center Test didn't work that way.

Mai had stealthily taken the test for real; official results weren't in yet, but her self-evaluation had left her with 830 out of 900. She'd managed 90 percent correct answers.

She'd talked like it was only normal to get a perfect score in your better subjects. Especially in math. Apparently, Sakuta was expected to get the first perfect score of his life on the Center Test next year.

Despite the abject nature of his results, Mai hadn't looked angry or even appalled. She'd smiled like a saint and said, "You love me, don't you?"

Which was way worse.

He would much rather get yelled at, scorned, and scolded. There was a real comfort in being directly told, "Study harder."

Perhaps he should be grateful she knew how to motivate him.

"In case you haven't noticed, I'll be a pal and clue you in."

Rio's voice pulled him back to reality.

He looked across the table; she had the tin of instant coffee open. She dumped a spoonful into a new beaker and poured in the water she'd boiled over the alcohol lamp. Steam rose up, carrying the scent of coffee in all directions.

"What?"

Was this a "give up while you still can" speech? No, Sakuta knew her better than that. It wasn't Rio's style. If she planned to discourage him, she'd have done it the first time he mentioned the idea of getting into the same college as Mai.

Stirring her coffee with a glass rod (intended for experiment use), Rio finally looked his way. Their eyes met for a brief second, then she looked at his hands.

"The problems you're looking at are for *high school* admission."

She sounded genuinely worried.

Sakuta followed her gaze, looking down. The energy conservation question was definitely something for the high school entrance exam. Converting potential energy to kinetic. Junior high science.

"So I'm concerned on *several* levels."

Behind her glasses, Rio's eyes filled with pity.

"I've gotta help Kaede study, so I need to review."

He snapped the book closed and dropped it on the lab table. The cover clearly stated it was a problem book for the prefectural high school exam.

"*That* is a huge relief," Rio said, taking a sip of her coffee.

"Futaba, you knew all along."

"I figured you weren't reading that by accident, but I couldn't completely rule out the idea that your foundation is so shaky you have to start over with junior high material."

Sakuta was intently watching her sip coffee, so she pushed the tin of instant coffee his way. Permission to help himself to the leftover hot water.

He hadn't been glaring at her out of desire for coffee, but it did seem like a good idea.

This can belonged to the physics teacher, so he had no compunctions about making himself an extra-strong cup.

It was a Friday, after six full periods of classes. January 23. It was four in the afternoon, and the baseball team was on the field, yelling. The science lab was well heated, and even instant coffee felt like a luxury. And they could boil water any time they wanted.

"But Kaede's gunning for a prefecture school?"

"Mm? Yeah, she wants to get into Minegahara."

"……"

That briefly silenced Rio. Likely a reaction based on full awareness of the admissions system. Without proper attendance, Kaede didn't have *grades*. And trying to get into Minegahara with that disadvantage...well, Rio was smart enough to know what that meant.

"That's a lot to handle."

"You've helped, too."

"......?"

She gave him a "What did I do?" look.

"You helped her study, right?"

"Over the summer? When I was staying at your place?"

For complicated reasons, she'd lived with them for a while.

"Yeah."

"But that was the other Kaede."

"She doesn't remember doing the studying, but she remembered what she learned."

So she was picking up math and science readily enough.

"Then you specifically came here to say that?" Rio asked, pulling tools for her next experiment out from under a desk.

"Nah, I had time to kill before my shift. And the coffee here is free."

"If you have time, spend it with Sakurajima."

"Mai left town yesterday to film a commercial. She's out today, too."

He was pretty sure she'd mentioned...somewhere in Nagasaki. She'd be home late tonight. What did people bring back from Nagasaki? He could only think of castella.

"Well, either way, glad this isn't more Adolescence Syndrome."

"Oh, about that..."

Her hands froze, and her gaze turned toward him. He awkwardly shifted his eyes until he looked out the window.

Rio sighed dramatically. "Azusagawa, you never learn."

It wasn't like he'd willingly participated in any of this, so that seemed unwarranted.

"This time, it's just a small thing bugging me. I don't think it's actually full-blown Syndrome."

He couldn't be totally certain of that, which was why he wanted her take on it. Couldn't hurt to ask.

"Really?" she said, skeptical. "Your instincts aren't exactly trustworthy here."

"I swear!"

"Then I guess I'll at least hear you out," she said. She looked annoyed but did ask, "So what happened?"

Her tone made it sound like she had experiments to do and wanted to get this over with, but he pretended not to notice.

"I had a dream about Mai, but she was a little kid in it. Think that means anything?"

He asked seriously, and Rio averted her eyes, sipping her coffee.

She sighed and then said, "A precursor to a one-way trip to the slammer." Very hostile.

"Fear not, I much prefer the current Mai."

A six-year-old in a red backpack did nothing for him.

"That statement does nothing to assuage my concerns."

"If I'm gonna dream about her, I'd far rather spend time with modern Mai."

"Wouldn't it be best to do that in real life?"

"An excellent suggestion, Futaba."

He fully planned on doing just that. Mai actually existed, and he was literally dating her. There was absolutely no need to seek fleeting comfort in dreams.

"But seriously, what do you make of it?"

He knew most people would assume it *was* just a dream. But Sakuta had good reasons to be less sure. Everything he'd been through made him aware that it could be a warning or a sign, or something already in progress.

"So what if it is?"

Rio seemed thoroughly uninterested.

"What if it's what?"

"Even if your dream is some sort of Adolescence Syndrome, it won't matter."

Her words sounded dismissive, but her tone had a breezy confidence.

"Because?"

"Whatever happens, you'll do something about it."

She glanced at him. Not joking or teasing. She genuinely thought that.

"You have far too much faith in me."

"I think you've earned it."

The more evasive he got, the more earnest she looked. He couldn't handle this. Didn't deserve it.

"Just look at what you've done already, Azusagawa."

"I barely did any of that on my own."

He wasn't even the one who'd created this timeline. That was a woman he'd looked up to. A girl he admired. Her courage had given him the happiness he currently enjoyed.

"You're more reliable than I'll ever be, Futaba."

With that, he downed the last of his coffee.

"Thanks for this," he said.

He still had time, but he decided to head in to work. If he talked to Rio any longer, she'd likely say something that made him squirm.

2

Sakuta left school a little earlier than planned and reached Fujisawa Station and the restaurant he worked at just after four thirty.

He said "Good morning" to the older lady working the register and headed in back to change. He was soon in his server uniform.

Once he was presentable, he returned to the break room, and the time card puncher still said four forty-five. Another fifteen minutes before his shift began.

Normally, he'd have killed this time just staring into space. But today, Sakuta was a new man.

"I guess I'd better."

He pulled his bag out of the locker and grabbed a book the size of a new hardcover. He brought that to the stool in the break room and sat down.

Sighing, he opened it. It was a book of English vocab. One thousand four hundred easy words. The book was brand-new. No crease in the spine. Mai had given it to him two days ago. She'd called after work and he'd gone downstairs to meet her, like a sucker, and she'd done her cutest smile and said, "I got you a present!"

Never for a moment suspecting it might be a vocab builder, he'd happily taken it.

"Learn all those in three months."

"That's…kind of a lot."

Just flipping through proved there were over three hundred pages.

"I'll be testing you every week to see if you've learned them properly."

"If I do well, is there a reward?"

"If you do poorly, there'll be punishment."

"That's honestly a fairly tempting offer."

Perhaps too much information. Mai gave him an extra-nice smile, and he concluded that he probably shouldn't joke around any further. Naturally, he'd meant every word, but…

So while helping Kaede study was important, Sakuta also needed to start the slow grind toward the college exam a year from now.

A year might seem like a lot, but if he didn't make smart use of these little pockets of time, he'd never pull it off.

His teacher had said most students started getting ready during summer of their second year. With his late start, he'd have to be that much more dedicated.

He had already committed the words on the first page to memory. The list of English words sat on the left, right alongside their respective meanings. On the right were example sentences using the words. Very easy to follow.

It came with a red plastic filter that would block out the red-ink definitions, allowing him to quickly check if he actually remembered things. Anything he didn't, he could review again in a flash, burning the words into his mind.

He repeated that, memorizing six pages. Maybe twenty words. Mai had set his target at a hundred words a week, so that was enough for one day...assuming he still remembered any of them tomorrow.

"I'll give 'em another once-over before bed."

He couldn't know what tomorrow would bring until tomorrow, so he'd just have to leave things up to himself then.

As that thought crossed his mind, he heard a door open and close outside the break room. Probably someone coming out of the girls' changing room.

A moment later, someone came into the break room itself. She passed right next to him, and he heard a slight intake of breath as she spotted him sitting there.

There was a long silence.

"...What are you doing, senpai?" she asked.

He knew who it was without looking. It might be a big universe out there, but only one person in it ever called him *that*. A first-year kohai from his school and a coworker at this restaurant, Tomoe Koga.

"What does it look like I'm doing?" he asked, not taking his eyes off the book.

"It looks like you're studying."

She spoke as if this was a mind-boggling wonder.

"That would be right."

"......"

He'd answered the question but sensed her voiceless query. He gave into his curiosity, looked up, and found her gaping down at him.

"That's a cute expression," he said. "What's wrong?"

"D-don't call me cute! And what's wrong with *you*?!"

"Nothing's wrong with me."

"You don't know?! You've really lost it!"

That sounded pretty rude. But they were always like this, so he didn't mind. Frankly, he was far more comfortable this way. It let him say whatever he felt, too.

"My academic skills are a lost cause, so I figured I'd better fix that."

He glanced at the time card clock; there were only two minutes left before his shift. He closed the vocab builder and stood up.

As he stuffed it in his locker, Tomoe's voiced drifted over the top of the rack.

"Are you going to college, then?"

"If I can get in."

Wishes alone would not get you there. You also needed considerable study skills and equivalent financing.

"You gonna still work here, or…?"

He shut the locker and emerged back into the break room. Tomoe had her lips pursed. Somewhere between a grump and a sulk. She quickly turned away.

"Not that I care," she said, ending the conversation.

She punched her time card, and his. Then headed out onto the restaurant floor.

Sakuta followed her, saying, "I'll still be working. Need the money."

"Right," she said, perking up a bit.

"Is that a smile?"

"N-no!"

She half turned toward him, cheeks puffed out.

"My financial struggles amuse you?"

"That's not why!"

"So you admit you were smiling?"

"I—I was not! Argh, you drive me nuts."

Sulking even harder, she spun around and headed over to bus a just-emptied table. He could hear her muttering away.

"Uh, Koga…"

"Do your job, senpai."

She was quickly stacking plates, stretching her petite frame out to reach the back of the booth and wipe it down.

"Before that, something important to discuss."

"What? Is this gonna be weird?"

Still fully stretched out, she turned her head in his direction, a look of deep suspicion in her eyes.

"Um, I guess in a sense? Yes."

"So what is it?"

His eyes slid down to her butt.

"That skirt's a bit tight, isn't it?"

"?!"

Tomoe quickly straightened up and spun toward him, hands clapped over her backside.

"It's giving you a VPL."

Not a problem if she was standing upright, but leaning over to wipe the table definitely tugged it flush against the rounded curve.

"Have you put on a few? Again?"

"I have not! And what do you mean, 'Again?'"

"You were griping about it after New Year's."

"Because you were mocking my puffy cheeks!"

"That's all?"

"And I lost four whole pounds! Look again!"

Tomoe glared at him.

"Still…," he said, his eyes dropping to her skirt. He was looking at her hips but only interested in her butt.

"Th-that's how it works!"

"How does what work?"

"S-sometimes you lose the weight and your butt doesn't shrink!"

Her face had gone all red, and she clearly objected to being forced to say any of this out loud.

"Oh. Well, it's very you, Koga."

"What definition of me is that based on?!"

"A butt-heavy one."

"You're the worst! I can't believe I'm still standing here!"

"You're the one contributing to the decline of public morals."

He pointedly glanced down again.

"Stop staring!"

Tomoe spread out her apron, blocking his view.

"You should talk to the manager, swap out for a size up."

"Never."

It was sound advice, rejected in a word.

"I'm sure my butt will catch up with the diet any day now. It's *gonna* shrink!"

"Then we'll have you focus on orders and the register today. Oh, look, table three's heading out."

A customer was heading for the register.

"I'll bus their table."

"You really are…"

Tomoe glared up at him. This definitely looked more like a sulk than anger.

"What?"

"Nothing."

She turned away, toward the register.

"Be right there!" she called, and she headed over, only slightly concerned about her backside.

He left seating customers, taking orders, and working the register to Tomoe and mostly busied himself with busing and setting empty tables, refilling paper napkins and glasses—all jobs that had him constantly in and out of the back.

After two hours spent earning his paycheck, it was just past seven, and he'd recently completed a round of the tables.

"Got a sec, senpai?" Tomoe asked.

"That was fast. Diet already fix your butt problems?"

"If you don't stop talking like that, someone's gonna press charges."

He turned around to find her scowling up at him.

"I'll be fine."

"The source of that confidence?"

"I only talk like this with you."

"I wish I hadn't asked."

Her cheeks were rather red.

"Nothing to blush about."

"I'm not!"

"Your cheeks seem to disagree."

"That's anger!"

"That kind of twitching is best left to butts."

"I swear I'm gonna slim down! And then I'll make you eat those words!"

She was somehow managing to look ashamed and furious at the same time.

"If that actually happens, sure."

How many times had Tomoe announced a new diet plan? He felt pretty sure she was telling him about a new one before he could tell if the last was working. In his mind, she was perpetually on a diet. That was her default state of being.

"Well, putting your weight aside..."

"You're the one who keeps bringing it up!"

"What did you actually want?"

"Oh, right. Over here."

She'd *clearly* forgotten, but she turned and headed toward the floor. When Sakuta just stood there, she beckoned.

"Hurry up!"

"What? Is there a customer so weird you've gotta show everyone?"

He followed her out and did a scan of the restaurant. He didn't see anyone particularly noteworthy. A group of four high school girls squealing about the latest romantic gossip. And a young couple occupying a four-top, a businessman with his laptop out, and a group of middle-aged men guzzling beers like this was a pub.

"I see nobody here who could possibly enrich my life in any meaningful way."

"She's outside."

Tomoe moved over to the register, glancing through the glass of the front doors. Sakuta followed her gaze and saw someone gingerly picking their path. All hunched over, to all appearances a bundle of nerves. She stopped just outside the doors, peering through like an animal on the lookout for threats. But before she could come in, another customer left, and she retreated to safety.

She had a coat over a long skirt, giving her a very bulky silhouette. Her hair was neatly cut just above the shoulders. She looked to be in junior high. Sakuta had not only seen her before, he'd seen her every day. They lived together. It was his own sister.

But that was exactly why it felt so strange to see her here.

He was left wondering just what the hell she was doing.

If it was really her at all.

It was that weird for her to venture out on her own.

Kaede had managed to start going to school earlier this year, but she still spent all the rest of her time cooped up in the house.

"She keeps almost coming in and then not. Should I, like, help?"

"I'll handle it. That's my sister."

"Huh? Your— Oh, right. You have one."

Tomoe kept squawking behind him, but Sakuta stumped right out through the doors to the outside. Kaede jumped at the sound of the doors opening.

"Kaede," he called.

She'd been cowering to the side, and she flinched at the sound of his voice, then turned slowly toward him.

"O-oh, Sakuta. Um. I was just…"

"You came all the way here alone?"

He got the answer to that before Kaede said anything. He saw someone hiding behind a car in the lot, watching over her.

Long, straight hair done up in braids today, with a pair of fake glasses to complete the disguise. Mai.

"Oh, Mai's with you?"

She must have gotten back from the commercial shoot.

"That sounded rude," Mai said, pretending to be cross. She came right up to him and pinched his cheek.

"Always glad to have you pamper me, even on the clock," he said.

He had to put his joy into words.

"Any seats open?" Mai asked, no emotion in her voice.

He'd wanted her to keep fussing, but she'd already let go of his cheek, her attention moving over his shoulder, checking how busy the restaurant itself was.

"Plenty," he said.

It was a comparatively slow day. Even on weekdays, there was often a waiting list between six and eight, but today he could seat them right away.

"Come on in," he said, opening the doors and waving them through. Tomoe handed him two menus, and he led them to the dining area.

Kaede followed after him, looking tense. Head not all the way up, constantly surveying her surroundings. Mai followed right behind her, hands on her shoulders for reassurance.

Sakuta took them to the booth at the very back. Once seated, almost nobody could see them.

"Will this table do?"

"Yes."

Once Kaede was sitting, Mai adjusted her own long skirt and took a seat herself.

"These are your menus," Sakuta said, putting one in front of each. "I'll just go fetch your waters," he said, and he stepped away.

He was soon back with two cups of water and a hot towel for each of them. He set them out on the table, and Mai thanked him with a smile. Kaede was curling into a ball. She kept glancing up and around. Clearly worried that other customers were looking.

Everyone was deep in their own conversations, paying her no mind at all.

"Being that nervous will just *draw* attention."

"I—I know, but…I've never been anywhere like this with anyone but Mom and Dad. I'm so out of my comfort zone…"

Kaede looked up at him, searching for guidance.

"Just sit back and relax. Even if anyone looks this way, they'll be looking at *Mai*."

"R-right. I knew that."

She sounded convinced but didn't straighten up at all. Like she was trying to make herself as small as possible.

"Don't worry, Kaede. Only a few customers can see into this booth. Right, Sakuta?"

Mai glanced his way, clearly aware of why he'd seated them here.

"Right you are."

That seemed to help, and Kaede's head finally came up. She opened the menu and flipped through it. Seeing all the photos of comfort food seemed to help relax her.

"So what brought this on?" he asked. The obvious question.

"Nothing," she said evasively. Eyes on the menu. Then she said, "Um…" and looked to Mai for help.

Mai had her menu open to the pasta section and said, "I'll have this, with this salad," pointing.

As Sakuta punched the order in, she added, "I brought over the Nagasaki souvenir and found Kaede there alone. She said you had a shift."

That left the bulk of the reason unstated but sort of made sense.

"Kaede said she hadn't eaten yet, and when I asked if there was anything she wanted, she said she wanted to see where you work."

"Oh yeah?"

He'd had no idea she was even curious.

"I-I've gotta turn in the application next week, right?"

"Uh, sure."

He felt like they'd skipped a transition.

"I have to take it to the school myself. I thought it would be good practice for going out."

Miwako had told him as much when she handed it over. Admissions would verify the applicant's identity then, so she would have to go in person. Shockingly, mailing it in was *not* allowed.

Sakuta must have taken care of that two years ago, but he had next to no memories of doing so. He'd probably just taken it to the office right inside the visitors' entrance, and it had all taken so little time it had left no real impression on him.

It had really been no big deal.

But for Kaede, going outside was *always* a big deal. She needed to train for it. If she couldn't turn in the application, she couldn't take the test. That was a bigger problem than studying for it.

"But you made it all the way here. Even if Mai did tag along."

"It was easier than going out in my uniform. There were lots of people by the station, and that was intense, but…"

Kaede smiled, putting a brave face on. And he only knew one thing to say to that kind of earnestness.

"Good work."

"Th-thanks."

Sakuta's praise earned another smile. This one wasn't forced—just a pure reflection of how she felt. But it was soon followed by a wave of awkwardness, and Kaede turned back to the menu, focusing on what to order.

"And thanks for coming with, Mai."

"You're welcome."

"Kaede, ready to order? It's on me," he said.

She was flipping back and forth between the page of omelet rice dishes and the list of parfaits.

"It's dinner time, so better go with actual food."

"I was just *looking* at the parfaits!"

She flinched, her voice shrinking. The gleam in her eye had made it clear she was doing more than looking. He went ahead and added the omelet rice to the pasta and salad.

He repeated the order back—by the book—bowed, and left their table. There were plenty of other customers, so he couldn't chat with them all night.

When he brought their food over, Kaede was busy studying.

She had a notebook out and a book of math problems open, and Mai was teaching her how to handle functions.

"Your food has arrived," Sakuta said.

Kaede jumped and looked up.

"Your omelet rice," he said, holding up the plate.

Kaede shoved the open books out of the way, making room for him to set it down. The fluffy yellow of the eggs glistened, and the demiglace sauce gave off a tantalizing odor.

"That looks *good*," Kaede whispered.

He set Mai's pasta and salad down, too.

"Dig in, Kaede."

"I—I will."

They both minded their pre-meal manners, then Kaede took a spoonful of omelet and the rice within. There was melted cheese hidden inside the egg, which also whetted the appetite. She scooped it all up and nervously took a bite.

She chewed a few times, and her lips curled up.

A look of pure bliss.

Feeling like that from eating a bog-standard dish at a chain restaurant meant Kaede was truly blessed.

She took another bite. As if remembering how good the first had been, this time she specifically took time to savor it. But her spoon never stopped. Her smile was infectious.

He was beaming from just watching her, and then he found himself remembering the other Kaede's smile. His other sister—she'd always smiled around him, always dedicated to the task at hand. He'd never been able to bring her here to eat this meal. He wished he could have.

He was sure she would've been delighted, probably grinning

ear-to-ear while she said something like "I think my cheeks fell off! Sakuta, are they still attached?!"

But that could never happen now. No matter how much he wished for it, he'd never hear her voice again. And the pain that caused him was proof that she'd been real, and a part of his life for the last two years.

That wasn't a regret. He wasn't racked by remorse.

This Kaede was steadily making progress between going out and working hard at her exam prep. And that just made the time the other one had spent with him that much more valuable. It was a happy thought, but also a sad one.

"Sakuta?"

"Mm?"

He blinked and found her looking awkwardly up at him.

"It's hard to eat with you staring at me," she said, shifting uncomfortably.

"Pretend I'm not here."

"That's impossible and wouldn't help. You seem strangely out of it, and it's super weird."

"Oh? I'm basically always like this. Right, Mai?"

Acting like nothing was out of the ordinary, he turned to Mai for comfort.

And found her mid-pasta-slurp. She reached for a napkin and dabbed her lips before answering.

"Yes. Sakuta is *always* like this."

Solid backup, but weirdly demoralizing.

"……"

Kaede seemed unconvinced. She was studying him intently.

"Wait, are you...?" she began, then broke off, staring at her hands.

"What?"

"...Never mind. Uh...are you working the next couple of days, too?"

A transparent attempt to change the subject. Her eyes were on her half-finished food. As she scooped up more chicken and rice, she looked a little downcast.

The next couple of days were a Saturday and a Sunday.

"Got an afternoon shift both days."

"Oh…"

"So we'll be studying in the evenings."

Kaede nodded wordlessly.

"Then you can study with me during the day," Mai suggested.

"Oh? You're off?"

"The filming dates shifted. So I've got the whole weekend off. I was hoping Sakuta had time for a date, but it sounds like he's busy with work."

Mai tilted her head to one side, looking up at him pointedly. The gesture seemed significant. Maybe she'd seen through his lie. And because he'd picked up on that, he didn't dare look away.

"Wish I hadn't taken these shifts, then."

He put on a sad face. Any blown date opportunity was tragic, so there was real emotion behind it.

"Um, then I'd love your help," Kaede said, looking nervous.

"I'll be there," Mai said, smiling warmly.

Kaede's nerves faded. And with that, Sakuta left their table.

A customer was waiting to pay, so he took over the register. Tomoe was busy delivering food.

"Exact change it is. Please come again!"

He watched them escort their kids out, and Tomoe caught up with him.

"Senpai, you're not working Sunday."

She was close enough that no one else could hear.

"What, Koga, were you eavesdropping?"

"I wasn't *trying* to snoop."

She shot him a disgruntled look. Her cheeks puffed out again.

"You shouldn't talk about poop in front of people."

"Ugh, so gross."

She radiated pure disgust. A very hostile look, but not nearly hostile enough. Your average high school girl just couldn't match Mai's intensity in that department. Sakuta regularly got bone-chilling stares out of her, and by comparison, Tomoe's were lukewarm water.

"Why'd you lie to your girlfriend and sister?"

"'Cause some things they're better off not knowing."

Like Tomoe said, Sakuta didn't have a work shift that Sunday. He'd originally had one, but something had cropped up, and he'd swapped with Yuuma.

"Are you cheating?"

Tomoe looked at him like he was filth.

"I'm dating the cutest girl in the whole world. Why would I waste my time doing something like that?"

"The fact that you're being completely serious just makes it worse."

Tomoe rolled her eyes at him. Was this what "teenage apathy" referred to? Sakuta hadn't been trying to make her laugh or anything. He'd just spoken the truth as he knew it, which might well be the objective truth, and perhaps that was why her smile looked strained.

"Fine, I'll buy you a *tantan-men* set if you keep silent."

This was one of the bigger meals on the menu. It came with two chicken nuggets and rice.

"That's the highest-calorie meal we have!"

"That's how we keep you being yourself, Koga. Calories."

"Senpai, you're gonna have to let me punch you."

"Oh, I actually have a favor to ask you."

"Wh-what?" She braced herself.

"Get a strawberry parfait started."

This was a seasonal special. It had a lot of strawberries in it and was the very thing Kaede had been eyeing intensely.

"Also mad calories!"

"It's not for you."

"Then who?"

"Take it to my sister's table once she's finished her omelet rice. I'll add it to the order."

He already had his pad out and was punching it in.

Kaede had worked hard to get here, and it was a small reward. Couldn't hurt.

3

Two days later. Sunday, January 25.

He told Kaede he was off to work and left at nine AM, with the sun barely risen.

He took the ten-minute walk to Fujisawa Station. With three lines headed through it, it was busy even on a day like this.

The restaurant he worked at was on the far side of the station from his apartment, but his feet stopped in front of the station building.

He used his train pass at the gates to the Odakyu Enoshima Line and stepped onto the platform. There was a rapid express bound for Shinjuku waiting on the first line, so he walked all the way down and boarded at the far end.

On a weekday, it would be packed with commuting office workers and students. On a Sunday, there were plenty of seats left, and he found one right away.

When it was time, the bell rang, and there was a hiss as the doors closed.

As the train pulled away, Sakuta opened his bag and took out the vocabulary book. He was memorizing the contents one page at a time. After a few pages, he used the red filter to hide the definitions and review. If he remembered everything, he moved on; if he didn't, he went back and started over.

He kept that up for a good hour, getting through forty pages of words. Then the train finally reached Shinjuku, the end of the line.

He put the book away and got off.

Crowds to his right and crowds to his left.

He found a sign, checking the directions to the south gate exit.

As he neared that destination, the lady he was meeting saw him across the gates. She had on a pastel jacket and a matching tight skirt. Like a fashionable mom at school for teachers' day. This was Kaede's school counselor, Miwako Tomobe.

"Find your way okay?"

"It's a single train."

"I mean in the station. You deliberately miss the point sometimes, don't you? This way."

She was laughing, though. Without waiting for an answer, she walked off. Outside the station, she headed toward Yoyogi. Sakuta followed, saying nothing. The crowds were dense enough that it was hard to walk side by side.

He finally caught up with her once she turned onto a back road.

"Thanks for joining me on your day off."

"No problem," she said. "I wanted to attend the orientation anyway, so your request was actually quite helpful."

This was why he'd spent a whole hour riding in here.

An orientation…

But not for Minegahara High.

One of the remote-learning centers Miwako had suggested the last time they met.

"It would really be best if Kaede came herself."

"Of course it would. But you want her focused on the prefectural exam, right?"

"Weren't you against her taking that, Ms. Tomobe?"

"As a school counselor, yes."

Miwako gave him a sidelong look, then smiled sheepishly. She hadn't wanted to be mean about it. But grown-ups sometimes had to say the realistic thing.

If Kaede could get into the school of her choice, Miwako knew that was best. If she could fit in at a normal school and enjoy her time there, then great. She thought both those things but also knew what she *had* to say, and she clearly voiced her objection.

"And that's why we trust you, Ms. Tomobe."

"Thanks. Your saying that makes me feel like I'm actually helping."

When there was a break in traffic, they crossed the street. Sakuta didn't know his way around, so he was simply going where Miwako went.

"Kaede's making good progress with her studies?"

"She's working hard. Was up late last night, too."

She'd been studying when he got back from his shift, and the date changed before she'd stopped. He'd made a late-night *onigiri* snack around ten, but when one AM rolled around, her light was still on.

At two, he'd finally said something—and there was no answer. He'd opened the door and found her asleep on her desk.

He'd somehow managed to pry her free and put her to bed, then went back to his room and slept himself.

"Worried she's trying a bit too hard, really."

There wouldn't be much point if she got sick on the big day.

"Then you should probably talk to her."

"She's not gonna listen."

Being dedicated and diligent was extremely important to Kaede right now. The downsides were obvious, but Sakuta was sure that discouraging her would benefit nobody.

There was value in letting her do things her way, as she saw fit, and finding out where that got her. If someone told her not to and she gave up before getting anywhere, she'd never achieve anything on her own. It would take away her chance to learn how to dig in when she needed to. And he didn't want Kaede to lose that.

"And that's why you're supporting her choice?"

He felt Miwako's eyes on him. Scanning his face. Testing him.

"You think she'll get in?" she asked, taking it one step further.

"I hope she can," he said, not backing down.

"You really never give anyone the answer they want, do you?"

But she was laughing pretty hard, shoulders rocking.

"I'm sure you know how difficult it'll be for her."

"Yeah."

"You just think unless she takes a run at it and sees where it takes her, she'll be stuck on it for ages?"

Sometimes your head understands the harsh reality, but your emotions refuse to fall in line. If you don't try—and fail—you never stop clinging to maybes. No matter how slim the chances, human emotions are always snarled up in hope.

And once those feelings take hold, you can't just let go of the possibility, not until you've done something. Not until you've at least *tried*.

That wasn't just true for Kaede. It was how Sakuta did things.

Realistically speaking, trying to get into Minegahara might be a futile effort. But she *wanted* this, and Sakuta had to respect that.

He didn't know if that was the right thing to do. Maybe it wasn't. But he felt sure it was better than just doing what the grown-ups said you should do, especially when you weren't remotely convinced they were right. He figured that making her own choices, stumbling, and picking herself back up would be valuable experiences and help Kaede in the future.

"The result may hurt her."

"Then I'll be real nice."

"So you're prepared to handle the fallout."

"I dunno about that, but I can do what brothers always do."

"I think you do a lot more than most boys your age could. Are you sure you're a teenager?"

"Of course. I'm a fresh-faced high school second-year."

"I don't think any real teenagers call themselves 'fresh-faced.'"

It *was* a boomer word.

"You're a good brother, Sakuta," Miwako said, still laughing.

"If I was any good, I wouldn't need your help here."

"You ever think about being a teacher?"

That came out of nowhere.

"Hah?"

He didn't mean to react quite that hard, but it *was* a pretty huge leap.

"You're going to college, right? Why not aim for a teaching license?"

Miwako was just pressing right ahead, heedless of his confusion. She seemed to think this was a totally natural conversational progression.

"Why me?"

"I think you'd be good at it."

She made that sound obvious, but it sure wasn't to him.

"Never."

"Why not?"

"Sounds like a huge pain."

What could be worse than trying to get through to students who wouldn't listen?

"Is there a job you'd rather do?"

"I was planning on leeching off my girlfriend."

"Ah, the gigolo life. That does seem very *you*," she cackled.

He'd been joking, but Miwako sounded weirdly convinced.

"Oh, wait up, Sakuta."

"Enough about my future."

"Not that. This is the school."

She stopped in her tracks. They were outside a standard commercial building; the first floor housed a café and a soba restaurant. It was made of red brick and was maybe three or four stories tall.

It didn't look like a school at all, but the class door had a SCHOOL ORIENTATION VENUE sign taped on it.

They stepped into the extremely un-school-like building. Still deeply unconvinced this was the right place, he and Miwako rode the elevator to the third floor.

There, they found a sign saying THIS WAY TO THE ORIENTATION with a big arrow on it, pointing them down the hall to the right. A dozen yards down the hall, they saw a big open room, brightly lit by fluorescent lights.

A young woman in a suit was at the door. "Right over here," she called with a pleasant smile. She looked to be in her midtwenties. Her name tag read *Instructor*, but she sure didn't look like a teacher.

"Sit right here," she said, leading them to a pair of empty seats. "We'll be getting started in approximately ten minutes."

And with that, she headed back to the door.

"Awfully young for a teacher."

"Your type?"

Miwako was teasing him again, so he ignored the question.

"Our school's staff is mostly middle-aged. Must be nice."

He made sure to keep his voice emotionless.

Maybe it was the lack of age gap, but that instructor hadn't felt uptight in any way. But she wasn't *too* friendly, either. She was welcoming a new family now, maintaining exactly the right level of warmth.

Sakuta and Miwako were seated at a long desk built for three. A man in his forties and a boy Kaede's age sat down next to them.

This hall was a good three to four times the size of a normal classroom, and there were maybe thirty pairs in that age range. Mothers or fathers with their kids, boys and girls.

All the kids looked like totally ordinary junior high school students. Stuck in a new place with their parents, not sure where to look. It didn't feel like the kind of room where you could start futzing with your phone, so they were all sitting still. Age-appropriate immaturity and stress levels showed on their faces.

But if they were *here*, they must all have had some reason why they might need to consider a remote-learning option, good or bad.

And that's why the room's silence seemed to have an extra layer of tension.

As Sakuta looked around, the ten-minute wait sped right on by. The clock hands hit the hour on the dot.

And the young woman who'd seated them stepped forward.

"It's time, so let's get this orientation underway," she said.

There was a stir as everyone sat up.

"We'll begin with a greeting from the principal. He'll be explaining how our school was founded and the principles upon which it operates. Mr. Tarumae, if you'd be so kind?"

The young woman bowed, and a man in a dark gray suit stepped forward. At a glance, he looked pretty young, but there were a few gray hairs there—probably late forties or early fifties.

He took the microphone and bowed to the crowd. He made sure it was turned on, then raised it to his lips.

"Thank you for attending today's orientation. My name is Tarumae, and I'm the principal here."

With that straightforward opening, he began by explaining that this school had opened a mere two years before. He made it clear they were still working out the kinks and had no intention of trying to hide that fact.

He was perfectly aware that their lack of clear results was a source of concern for potential students and parents.

But with that in mind, he proceeded to make the case that the school's newness was both an asset and a selling point.

"Because we're a new school, because we're so young, we believe we are well equipped to create an educational program aligned with this day and age. Things are changing all the time. Twenty years ago, nobody could have imagined how online we'd all be, that we'd all have smartphones in our pockets. Today, if we don't understand something, we can just look it up. We can easily do our shopping no matter where we are. We can stay in touch with friends and family over social networks. Our lives have changed dramatically in the past two decades. But has school? The way we teach has barely changed. Not since your parents' time. Not since their parents' age. Both now and then, educational approaches have remained static. That's just 'how it's done.' How 'everybody does it.' And nothing ever changes. Conventional schools cram thirty or forty kids in a classroom, running through the same lectures at the same times every single day. Even though those thirty or forty kids have thirty or forty different personalities and comprehension skills. Naturally, there are people who thrive in that environment. It's just a fact that some students were built for conventional schooling. We have no intention of discrediting that approach. We simply want to offer additional options for further education. New educational approaches. The school of the future. And this institution was founded to do just that."

Occasionally slowing to choose his words, or rephrasing when he felt an expression was lacking, the principal spoke on, eyes focusing on one future student or parent after another. Sakuta included.

"Our school provides all the basic education required for a high school diploma but allows each student to learn it at their own pace. Our classes are prerecorded videos that can be watched on your computer or phone, so students can learn at home, the café, or a family restaurant. Our specialized curriculum allows students to graduate by watching lectures for only an hour and a half a day and completing relevant assignments. There is no need to spend half of every day cooped up in a school building, and the students are always in control of their own progression speeds."

Sakuta was jealous already. An hour and a half at Minegahara would mean going home after second period.

"I'm sure there are students and parents who are wondering if they can maintain that discipline, but rest assured, you *do* have teachers monitoring your progress, even remotely. When your homework deadlines approach, they will be using phones and e-mail to stay in touch. With our video learning system, your instructors are not conducting classes. But that gives them more time to communicate with each student on an individual basis. And they talk about more than just study progress; they're happy to discuss all kinds of things, up to and including the student's hobbies and passions."

That certainly explained the warm vibe the teacher who'd seated them had. If she spent every day talking to students about their lives, you would wind up a good deal closer to them compared to normal teachers.

And that teacher was standing by the principal, nodding emphatically.

"By allowing them to acquire the knowledge necessary for graduation at their own pace, we give them additional time for what they really care about and let them try their hands at elective fields of study. If you're interested in English, we have short-term study abroad programs. If you're looking to get into an elite university, we have a specialized curriculum prepared in tandem with a prep school. We have courses on fashion, design, cooking, and programming, all provided through partnerships with specialty schools. Providing this new system of learning allows today's children to learn the skills they need for the lives they want. We believe it is the way of the future."

From what he'd said, it wasn't at all clear what parts of the program were working and what parts weren't. But there was a lot to agree with in the philosophy he'd outlined. A school that changed with the times and with the students' individual needs.

Sakuta remembered that Miwako had talked about how there were always students who couldn't fit in at school, in class, in those social systems. Everyone knew that, yet they still forced everyone into the same classrooms, gave them the same lectures, and had them attend the same functions. Perhaps that *was* because educational methodology wasn't evolving with the times.

The idea that those who couldn't fit in were to blame was definitely backward, and it made no sense that your life hinged on whether you could adapt to the current approach.

Social groups unconsciously generated malice and pressure, invisible to the naked eye but no less real. And the hormone-fueled environment of a school class was extra potent.

Everyone had long since worked that out, but nothing had been done. One false move, and anyone could end up like Kaede. Buffeted by jeers from your "friends" until you stopped going to school, stopped thinking you could do what everyone else did. Once that happened, it was no small task to pick yourself back up. It took a ton of courage and willpower. Yet few could understand that agony.

Nobody could understand until it happened to them.

"That's all from me. Next we'll be showing you a video that features the voices of students who've completed a year with us. What could be better than hearing it direct from the source?"

And with that, he nodded at the female instructor. There was a large screen on the wall, connected to a laptop.

Cheery music played, accompanying a video about the school itself.

It began with the same things the principal had just enthused about. Why the school was founded, how credits were earned, an average student's schedule. After that, it was just what the principal had said—interviews with real students.

Q: After a year here, how do you feel?

The question appeared silently on-screen.

"At first, I wasn't into remote learning or online classes. I thought, 'That's not a real school.'" The speaker was a uniformed boy with short hair. "But we've got uniforms and morning homeroom, and the teacher takes attendance every day in the chat room. We don't *have* to be there every time, but it's become part of my routine. In the beginning, I just watched other students talk, but slowly I started to join in. Even made some friends."

He seemed pretty tense at first, but by the end, there was a smile on his face, albeit a sheepish one. Especially on the last line.

The video moved right along, switching to the next student. A smaller boy, with glasses.

"We can make clubs, too. When I first started, it was just someone I met in chat who was into the same things. It turned out we both played instruments, so we figured we might as well start a band. We found enough people that we're thinking about playing a concert. We live all over the place: Kanagawa, Chiba, Saitama, and Hokkaido. We all got jobs so we could go visit the Hokkaido member. It was the first time we'd all met up in person, but we'd been talking online so much, it was really easy to adjust. We're gonna meet up again soon."

Next up was a studious-looking girl. She was really into English, and wanting to improve it, she'd done the short-term study abroad program that summer and apparently had a very good time. She said, "I want to go back!" and added, "But maybe I'll try a different place next summer," as she leaned forward.

The video was an ad for the school, so naturally, it was all positive. But everyone interviewed was clearly excited about their time here and eager to share. None of it rang false.

Sakuta could never talk like this about Minegahara. If he was asked about life there, he would never speak with this *glow*.

At best, he'd mention the view. That they weren't too strict with the students. And that *the* Mai Sakurajima went there. There wasn't much else to write home about.

As these thoughts ran through his mind, another girl showed up on-screen.

Long black hair. Tall and slim. She had her legs crossed, and her back was bolt upright.

Mm? Sakuta thought. She looked familiar. But he couldn't quite place her.

"I started out at a conventional school. But I never really found a place in the social circles there, so I didn't last long."

That was rather grim, but she seemed fairly upbeat. And there was a distinctive bounce to her voice that finally helped Sakuta connected the dots.

She was in the same idol group as Nodoka, Sweet Bullet. At the concert he'd been to, she'd been in the center, getting the most attention. Her name was Uzuki Hirokawa. The fans called her Zukki.

He had a *vivid* recollection of her midskit claim that idols don't wear panties. It was a hard thing to forget.

"People are forever telling me I don't know how to read the room, so

I ended up all on my own. I mean, rooms don't have any words—what is there to read? Come on! So school got boring fast, and going every day was a chore. Halfway through the year, I'd completely stopped going, but then I heard about this place, and it sounded neat. So I quit my old school and swapped over! Now I've got friends. They tell me the *same* things, but here, people just think it's funny."

She laughed merrily. It wasn't only her. Everyone in these interviews was happy and having fun, eyes sparkling. Full of hopes and dreams.

Uzuki was the closer, and the screen soon faded to the ending music.

When orientation ended and Sakuta and Miwako left the venue, the sun was high above. It was twelve thirty.

They headed back the way they'd come, to Shinjuku Station.

"What did you make of it?" Miwako asked.

"Seems like the kinda school a pantyless idol would choose."

Thanks to Uzuki's last-minute appearance, Sakuta's impression of the school was irrevocably tied to her.

"A what now?" Miwako said, puzzled. As well she might be. It was a statement that required context.

"Uh, never mind," he said. "It was certainly not what I expected."

That was his main takeaway. It was the exact opposite of what he'd assumed *remote learning* implied. It seemed full of vim and vigor.

"What the principal said seemed like good stuff. It made sense to me, anyway."

"I'm definitely in favor of adapting educational approaches to fit the times. And new schools have less red tape and are able to tackle that approach better."

New ways of learning.

A school built for today.

It was hard to tell how much of that was practical and how much of it idealized. But the core principles and desire to put them into practice was something Sakuta could respect.

He felt like the trip had been worth it just to know a place like that existed.

Now he and Kaede would just have to figure out what to do, even as they prepped for the prefectural exam.

4

Miwako had other business in the area, so they split up at the station, and Sakuta spent an hour riding back to Fujisawa.

Naturally, he filled the time with English vocab.

It was past two by the time he reached his destination. He stopped in the electronics store, browsed the bookstore, and killed a little more time before heading home.

Since he'd lied about having a shift today, he couldn't get home *too* early.

After a ten-minute walk from the station, he reached his apartment building.

"I'm home," he called as he stepped in.

A pair of shoes sat at the entrance. Not his or Kaede's. Girls' shoes, the heels neatly placed together.

They belonged to Mai.

He locked the door, took off his shoes, and poked his head into the living room.

"I'm back," he said again.

"Hey," Mai said softly. She pointed at Kaede, who was sound asleep on the *kotatsu*. "She was up late studying last night. I figured it was time for a break and some tea, but the moment I looked away, she was out like a light."

Mai had two cups ready in the kitchen.

"She's been pushing it. Make sure she sleeps right."

Kaede working hard was a good thing, but it would never do if she made herself sick. And trying to study while nodding off wasn't very effective.

"Got anything to cover her with? I don't want her getting chills."

"There's a blanket in her room."

"Good idea."

Mai wasted no time, heading right on in and coming back with a small blanket. She gently laid it on Kaede's shoulders, making sure not to wake her.

Sakuta went to his own room to change.

He put his bag on his desk and took off his clothes, top and bottom, leaving him in his drawers.

And just as he got to that stage, there was a knock on the door.

"Coming in, Sakuta."

Before he could say anything, Mai opened the door and stepped in. When she saw him nearly naked, she rolled her eyes at him, closing the door behind her.

"Get dressed," she said, exasperated.

"I must protest, Mai."

"What?"

"You're the one who opened the door before I answered."

"True."

"Eek," he deadpanned.

Mai utterly ignored this, sitting down on the edge of the bed. The very bed upon which he slept.

Was that a sign she was good to go? He rather hoped it was, but instead, she put a bored look on and said, "Have fun at work?"

"Uh, no? It was real busy—need you to comfort my weary bones."

He opened the closet to fetch some clothes. He took out some sweatpants and a long-sleeved T-shirt and sensed her gaze on him. He turned back toward her.

"What?"

"So where'd you actually go?" Mai asked, legs crossed.

"What do you mean, 'actually'?" he tried.

"Instead of this lie you're telling me about a shift at work."

Her tone was getting frostily polite. He couldn't tell how sure she was, but her expression and tone made it sound like she wasn't just fishing. She seemed like she already knew.

That alone meant nothing. She'd been an actress most of her life.

And there was no point trying to match her talent, so he just took the orientation pamphlet out of his bag.

"This."

He handed it to Mai.

"Ah," she said, glancing down at it. But then she looked back up, glaring at him. "But why was it a secret from me?"

"I didn't want to make you have to lie, too."

"But I'm better at it?"

He wasn't talking about technique here. Mai was well aware of that but phrased it like that anyway. That left him without an escape.

"Okay, I didn't want it to be *just* Kaede who's been in the dark. That's why I kept it from you, too."

This was the honest truth, but it only deepened her frown.

"If you put it like that, I can't torment you."

"Since you're such an accomplished liar, pretend you never knew about this."

"Fine. When it comes time to tell her, I'll be on her side, and we'll torment you together." Mai was finally smiling. But then she asked, "So when are you gonna tell her?"

She handed him back the pamphlet. He took it and returned it to his bag. Best if Kaede didn't see it yet.

"I want her focused on the prefectural exam, so after that."

"It's gonna hurt."

Mai glanced at the door, toward where Kaede slept.

"She wants you fully in her corner. You'll be in the doghouse for a while."

But *somebody* had to plan for contingencies. And while she was busy studying, that had to be him.

"I'll need you to comfort me, then."

"Can't. I just promised to take her side."

"Aww."

"I couldn't bear losing Kaede." Mai smiled, clearly joking.

"Mai, I want you thinking only of me."

"I always am."

She got up from the bed and stepped closer to Sakuta. Her hand came up, and the tips of her fingers touched his chest.

"I'm glad the scars are gone."

"Mm?"

"On your chest."

Three big claw marks running from his right shoulder to his left side. Adolescence Syndrome resolved, the issue causing them was gone, and Sakuta was no longer visibly scarred.

"I feel like less of a man without the wild vibe they gave me."

"Fair."

They could joke now *because* it had all ended well.

"You'll make yourself sick standing around without a shirt on."

"But we haven't even done anything yet!"

A hint of a smile crossed Mai's lips, and she ran her fingers down where the scar had been.

"Ohhh!"

It tickled, and he made a weird noise.

And just as he did…

"Sakuta, you're home…?"

…the door opened.

Kaede poked her head in through the half-open door and froze. Her eyes had found them. Sakuta in his underwear and Mai's fingers stroking his chest.

"……"

There was a solid two-second pause, and then Kaede quietly shut the door.

"Kaede! We're not—"

It was rare to hear Mai yelp like that. She ran out after Kaede.

He could hear her muffled voice yelling "I swear!" through the door.

Sakuta finally put some clothes on.

5

As January drew to a close, the temperatures got that much gnarlier. The weather report yesterday had said, "Cold flowing down from the north will make it chilly enough for scattered snowflakes, not just along Kanto's northern mountains, but in the flatlands to the south and along the coasts."

That forecast had proved unusually accurate. Sakuta lived on the coast at the southern end of Kanto, but there were definitely tiny snowflakes in the air.

Afternoon and fifth-period math rolled around with no signs of the snow stopping.

Sakuta sat by the window, so he could easily tell how cold it looked. On a clear day, this seat gave him a magnificent view of the sea, sky, and horizon. Today he had a rare glimpse of snow falling on the ocean, as far as the eye could see.

But Sakuta was not in the mood to enjoy that winter wonderland. The clock had all his attention. He'd been checking at least every three minutes since fifth period started.

When the teacher finished explaining an example integral problem, Sakuta made sure he had everything in his notes and checked the clock again.

It was almost two PM.

Probably the right moment for it.

So he raised his hand, calling the teacher's name. Chalk in hand, they turned toward him—as did the eyes of every classmate.

"Yes, Azusagawa?"

"Can I go to the bathroom?"

"Hold it."

"Can't."

"Then go on."

Permission granted, he got up. As he passed the board, he said, "It's a number two, so it might be a while."

"Too much information," the teacher grumbled.

His classmates' laughter still ringing in his ears, Sakuta left the room.

With classes in session, the halls were eerily quiet. The faint drone of teachers' voices through the doors, the sounds of students scribbling notes or shifting in their seats. A manufactured hush.

Sakuta's footsteps felt extra loud.

He was alone in the halls. That was kind of a rush, but there was a grain of guilt hidden within. He walked *right* past the men's room.

And down the stairs.

Not because the faculty toilet was better suited to giant dumps.

He sailed past the main entrance, heading for the side of the school, where the visitors' entrance lay. Over by the main office.

The reception window was open, and a fortysomething female faculty member was on duty. They did not normally have anyone sitting in this window, but the sign saying APPLICATION COUNTER made it clear why someone was there today.

It was January 29. The prefectural high school application window had started yesterday, and it closed tomorrow.

Sakuta had been keeping one eye on the time because this was when Kaede had planned to hand in her application.

Neither she nor anyone her age was anywhere to be seen. Miwako had said this was the eye of the storm and the least popular time to turn anything in; clearly, she'd been right.

Afternoon on day two.

Most students either got it over with on the first day or fretted about it till the last second and came running in on day three.

After talking it over with Kaede, they'd agreed she should bring hers by today. The fewer people she ran into, the better.

"Excuse me."

"Yes?" The lady at the window gave him a searching look. He was definitely not supposed to be wandering around the halls while classes were in session.

Before she could start to pry, he asked, "Has Kaede Azusagawa turned in her application yet? She's my sister but has been out of school awhile. I'm worried she won't even make it here."

Best to just tell the truth here. He pulled his student ID out of his jacket pocket, proving he was really a student here and his name really was Sakuta Azusagawa.

The faculty lady was clearly a bit taken aback but got why he was concerned. "Just a minute," she said and riffled through the stack of applications she'd received. "She hasn't shown up yet."

"Thanks for checking."

He left the reception window and went out the visitors' entrance, still in his school slippers.

Sticking to the roofed area, he looked toward the gate. There were three people her age with umbrellas there, but he could tell none of them were Kaede. All were wearing pants.

"Can she really do this?"

When he'd left the house that morning, he'd definitely asked if she could make it all the way to Minegahara on her own, but she'd insisted she could do it.

He wanted to believe in her. To respect her choice. She'd spent the last few days in an indignant huff, which certainly didn't inspire confidence.

Ever since she'd caught him flirting with Mai on Sunday, Kaede had clearly been in a mood.

They were still eating breakfast and dinner together, and she was still asking for help with her studies, but the look on her face suggested she was still holding it against him.

He waited for Kaede a while longer, but she didn't show.

Wanting a better look, he left the roofed area and headed toward the school gate. He didn't have an umbrella, and the snow was getting all over his uniform. It was snowing much harder than it had looked through the window. Each individual flake was tiny, so it wasn't really accumulating on the ground, but it was enough to turn Sakuta's shoulders white.

The wind was bitterly cold. He fought off the urge to flee back to the warmth of his classroom and peered around the gate.

The bells at the crossing were ringing. Train coming. He could see it pulling out of Shichirigahama, bound for Kamakura. Which meant it had come from Fujisawa. Kaede might have been on that.

The bells stopped.

Not long after, people coming from the station rounded the corner carrying umbrellas. They were junior high students in uniforms and winter coats. Six in all, keeping their distance from one another. They all entered through the gates and walked past Sakuta, each one with a tense look on their face.

Kaede wasn't with them.

"The next train, then?"

He sighed, making a white cloud. His fingers were going numb. At this time of day, the next train was twelve minutes off. Just as he was starting to consider going back inside, he saw a new umbrella round the corner. A plain, unadorned navy blue.

She had the umbrella held out before her, so he couldn't see her face. But he knew it was Kaede. She was wearing the coat Mai gave her over her uniform and had mittens on. And a scarf that matched those mittens. Black tights to stave off the snow's chill. It was the same look she'd shown him that morning.

One mitten held the umbrella, and the other was clutching a transparent plastic folder. Kaede kept stopping and checking the folder. It probably contained the map Sakuta had given her. Most people didn't print out maps these days, since they could pull them up on their phones, but Kaede's social life had collapsed after a phone-related squabble, and she still tensed up if she heard a ringtone, even on vibrate. She couldn't exactly carry one around with her.

She reached the little bridge before the crossing. She made it halfway across, then stopped dead in her tracks.

She'd spotted a uniformed girl coming back after turning in her application. Kaede didn't move another step until that girl was safely behind her.

After that brief hiccup, she set out again. But one returning student after another passed her, and each time, she hid beneath her umbrella.

"......"

It would be so easy to run over to her.

For him to help her turn in the application.

But watching her push herself here, one step at a time, he knew he shouldn't.

Sakuta retreated back inside before she saw him.

He passed a few kids coming back from turning their forms in. They saw him covered in snow and looked puzzled. One boy straight up gave him a head tilt. They must have thought he had a screw loose.

Sakuta didn't give a shit. He didn't care what they thought. The opinions of strangers never meant anything to him.

He wished he could share that mind-set with Kaede. But that was impossible, so he just went back to the office window and waited quietly for her to get there.

He shook the snow off his uniform, but still no Kaede.

Five minutes. Ten. No Kaede.

Sakuta grimly hung on, and at last she stepped in the visitors' entrance. She shook the snow off her umbrella. She found the sign for the application desk and looked relieved.

And then she saw him standing there.

"Huh?"

"Applications go right here."

"R-right."

He took the umbrella from her. She put the map folder away and pulled the application folder out—all with her mittens on. That was odd.

Still all gloved up, she moved closer to the window. Scarf still wrapped up tight, too.

"H-hi," she said, holding out the envelope with both hands.

"Hello. Let's see…you must be Kaede Azusagawa, yes?" the woman asked.

She took the form, glanced it over, and took a good look at Kaede's face.

"Th-that's right."

"We've received your application. Good luck on the test."

"Th-thank you."

Kaede bowed her head and left the window. She came trotting back to Sakuta.

"Why are you *here*?"

"I had to go to the bathroom, so I swung by."

"Are there bathrooms *outside*?"

"What makes you think that?"

"You've got snow all over you."

She was staring at the sleeves sticking out of his blazer. He'd brushed himself off, but there were still flakes hidden.

"These coastal winds are fierce."

She was still staring fixedly at him, so he reached out and patted her on the head.

"Huh? What's that for?"

"Good work getting here."

"I just turned in a form!"

But she definitely seemed pleased.

Not long ago, she could never have done this. And doing so gave her confidence.

"Then I'd better get home."

"Wait, Kaede."

"Wh-why?"

"Take the scarf off a sec."

"?!"

She didn't have to ask why. She flinched—and that was his answer.

He reached for the scarf's coil, and she grabbed his hands, stopping him.

"Don't!" she snapped.

But her elbow caught her sleeve, and he caught a glimpse of wrist between coat and mitten. Sickly-pale skin that had never seen the sun. And a faint bruise.

"No, it's not…," she said, stepping back and dropping her hands. She hid the wrist, shaking her head.

"Look, Kaede…"

"It's fine! It'll heal right up!"

There was desperation in her voice, and she kept denying it, but even as she did, the bruise spread up her neck to her chin.

"I can take the test! I can go to high school!" she said, on the verge of tears. "Don't…tell me I can't. I can work just as hard…!"

She looked up at him, scared.

It sounded like she was comparing herself to someone else.

Just as hard as…?

Who?

Everyone at her school who was actually attending class?

That didn't feel right.

He was pretty sure she was thinking of the other Kaede here. The one who'd spent two years working hard in her place.

"Kaede."

"…I can do this."

"Why do you want to come to Minegahara?"

He could guess.

"……"

So when she avoided his gaze and hung her head, he didn't press the point.

"Maybe that's not important. I chose it pretty much at random myself."

He reached out and lightly pinched her cheek.

"…Wh-what's that for?"

"Nobody said you couldn't."

"…Yeah?"

"If there's something you wanna do, I'm here to help you do it. No matter who says otherwise."

"......You swear?"

Kaede looked up at him, eyes glistening. He was still pinching her cheek, so this was pretty silly looking.

"I swear. But in return, don't hide the bruising from me."

"O-okay."

He'd known Kaede's Adolescence Syndrome had never fully gone away. He was well aware they'd have to beat it one step at a time. He'd had a feeling this would happen eventually the moment she said she wanted to take the exams.

"We're doing a full body check when we get home."

"Um. *You're* doing this?"

"If I don't, how will I know how far we can push things?"

"B-but, like..." She waved a hand. "It's embarrassing."

She'd turned pretty red and was muttering under her breath.

"Not like I'm gonna look up your nose."

"I-it's my *body* I don't want you seeing!"

"It's nothing to be embarrassed about."

"Sure, I'm nothing like *Mai*, but..."

She shot him a reproachful look. She definitely seemed a lot more relaxed now. The bruise on her chin was retreating like a wave on the beach. Sakuta was relieved to see that and finally let go of her cheek.

"Let's be clear, Kaede."

"A-about what?"

"You've got a lot of nerve even comparing yourself to Mai."

"I—I know that! But hearing it from you is just...argh!"

"Why?"

"Too many reasons."

She puffed out her cheeks, growling. It only made her look ridiculous, and he wasn't exactly shaking in his slippers.

"If you've got the energy to do the teenage-sister act, you oughtta be able to make it home alone."

"I *am* a teenage sister! So, uh. Just be more careful."

"Careful?"

"About *stuff*. Like what you were doing with Mai on Sunday."

She got redder and redder, and by the end of that sentence, her voice died away to a whisper. He could barely make out the last word.

"Fair. We'll save that for when you're not around."

"Don't even *talk* about it! I'm leaving!"

Clearly feeling much better, she snatched her umbrella from him and dashed out the visitors' entrance. He followed her as far as the roofed section.

"Thanks," she said softly.

"For what?"

"For the moral support. I'm glad you were here."

"Watch your step. You don't wanna slip up and *fail*."

"Don't say that to an exam student!"

She shot him an uneasy smile and then put her umbrella up, setting out into the snow. She turned back once a few yards out, smiled when she saw he was still watching, and then waved good-bye.

Kaede spent the next few weeks doing the groundwork for the test itself.

Weekday mornings she went to her junior high to study in the nurse's office. She came straight home after and studied more. Saturdays she spent the whole day hunched over her desk.

When she got stuck, she had Sakuta help, and when she was studying late, he'd make her a late-night snack. Mai and Nodoka stopped by when they had time and helped her study.

The fruits of her labors were apparent, and each time she went through a set of old test problems, she got a better score. If she had a proper transcript, she could easily have made it into Minegahara. Miwako seemed genuinely impressed by her progress.

February passed one day at a time, and each of those days was rewarding. Then the day of Kaede's battle arrived—Monday, February 16. The day of the prefectural high school exams.

Chapter
3

open the door

1

The morning dawned in a way that made Sakuta go, "Ugh, morning already?" before his alarm even went off.

Only his head and cheek were out of the comforter, but the air felt cold. He didn't wanna leave his cocoon. Losing the battle, he lowered his lids to go back to sleep…and *then* the alarm clock started screeching.

His hand shot out from the covers to turn it off, slapping the top of the clock. He managed to pry his eyes halfway open again, enough to focus on the digital display.

Six AM. February 16. Monday.

Far too early to get ready for school.

Normally, he'd have sworn at himself for setting his clock wrong and sunk back into a blissful slumber.

But today he fought off the allure of his warm bedding and sat up. He yawned once and rolled out of bed. His eyes were still only half-open, but that was enough to pick his way into the hall.

In the bathroom, he washed his face, then his hands. Even gargled.

He moved to the living room and found sun streaming through the gap in the curtains. There was a gurgling noise from the dimly lit kitchen. He glanced at the rice cooker and saw steam rising like an old locomotive.

Almost done.

Sakuta opened the curtains and went back to the kitchen. The light on the rice cooker switched from COOK to KEEP WARM.

Sakuta had washed the rice last night and set the time so it would cook in the morning.

He moved past the workhorse cooker over to the fridge. He took out an onion, peeled it, and chopped it up. He began sautéing it on the stove.

When it was golden brown, he grabbed a bowl, plopped in a mix of ground beef and pork, and stirred in milk, eggs, bread crumbs, and nutmeg. He dropped in the sautéed onions, gave it a twist of salt and pepper, and mixed some more.

Ready to cook.

After rolling the mix into bite-size balls, he coated the pan in oil and started frying.

The tantalizing aroma of browning meat filled the room.

When both sides of the balls were seared, he lowered the flame and put the lid on the pan. Now he just had to let it steam until they were cooked through.

He wrapped up the rest of the meat mixture and stuck it in the fridge. That would be his lunch.

Sakuta put another pan on the second burner. This one had four corners.

Once it had warmed up, he poured in beaten eggs and started rolling them. He moved the finished roll to a dish and sliced it into bite-size pieces.

He put the finished meatballs on the same dish.

The scent rising from them whetted his appetite, and he went ahead and popped a slice of rolled egg in his mouth. Savoring the hint of sweetness, he opened the rice cooker. A rush of steam rose up from the white grains.

He gave them a gentle stir with the rice paddle, put some cling wrap down on the table, and set aside some rice for *onigiri*.

He let that sit.

Once it had cooled a bit, he got out the pickled plums and pollack roe, then balled the rice up around them.

He wrapped the rice balls in seaweed and stuffed them in a two-layer bento box. Two *onigiri* filled the lower layer. In the top layer, he piled meatballs and rolled eggs, then added some lettuce and cherry tomatoes. He finished off the lunch with a scoop of the potato salad he'd made the day before.

"That should do it."

Sakuta sounded satisfied, but his work was not yet done. He put some sliced bread in the toaster, washed the frying pan, and melted some butter over a low heat. Once it was ready, he poured in some eggs he'd scrambled with milk.

He kept it moving with a spatula, mixing the eggs so they didn't cook too fast. They gradually solidified, staying nice and fluffy.

He turned off the flame before they got too hard and heaped the scrambled eggs onto a pair of plates. Next to that went some octopus-legged wieners.

The toast popped up nicely browned, so he put that on the plates as well and placed them on the table. Then he moved to Kaede's door.

"It's morning!" he called, opening the door. "Up and at 'em!"

Something shifted under the round pile of covers. There was a noise, but it was hard to tell if that was just noisy breathing or sleeptalk.

"You've got exams today. You can't be late."

That got through. Kaede's head popped out of the heap.

"What time is it?!"

"Seven."

"Oh...then I'm not late yet." She looked relieved. "Don't scare me like that!"

Kaede got out of bed, shooting him a look of protest. This was soon interrupted by a huge yawn. Her eyes were still bleary with sleep.

His gaze seemed to make her uncomfortable.

"I couldn't fall asleep last night," she admitted. He hadn't even asked, and she was already making excuses.

"What, were you excited about something?"

"It's the exam today! Argh, you knew that." Kaede screwed up her lips, disgruntled. "This is bad! What if I nod off during the exam?!"

"No big deal," he said, shrugging.

"It's a huge deal!" Kaede was getting more and more worried.

"Nobody there'll have slept much, I promise. Everyone's anxious and worried."

"You're sure?" She did not seem to find that comforting.

"Everyone's in the same boat."

"Well, okay. I'm just like everyone else, then."

She finally sounded convinced. There was a hint of a smile showing.

"Were you stressed out?" she asked.

"Yeah, so stressed out I had to make a bathroom run midtest."

"I think I would worry about that *more*."

"It was a number two, by the way."

"Gross!"

She stuck out her tongue and left the room. She saw breakfast on the table and let out a squeak of joy.

"Scrambled eggs! They look so good."

"Better wash your face before they get cold."

"Right…"

Kaede padded off to the bathroom. He heard water running, then the sound of her gargling…and when she came back, she was finally fully awake.

They sat down on opposite sides of the table and clapped hands.

Kaede grabbed her spoon and dug into the eggs. They were still piping hot. Fluffy and creamy.

Mai had taught him the trick to making them just right. She'd made them several times while she was over, and Kaede had swooned over them every time.

That was why he'd picked them for her exam breakfast. Anything to put her in a good mood as she headed out the door.

From the look on Kaede's face, his scheme had paid off. She was savoring every bite with a look of bliss.

"These are just like Mai's scrambled eggs," she said.

If a single meal was all it took to put her in the right frame of mind for a big day, then great. Waking up a bit early was worth it.

The one downside was that Kaede was eating extra slow. She was never exactly a fast eater, but she was trying to get the most out of every bite and was only halfway through her eggs by the time Sakuta finished his.

"Better eat up, or you really will be late," he said, carrying his dishes to the sink.

"It's a waste to wolf this down!"

If she could relax and enjoy her food, then he felt like she'd be okay for the test, too.

"If you like 'em that much, I'll make 'em tomorrow, too."

"But I *do* think Mai's are better," Kaede added.

Also a promising sign.

"Well, yeah. Mai's the best."

"……"

Spoon in her mouth, Kaede gave him a searching look.

"What, is there a ghost behind me?"

He made a show of looking over his shoulder but found only wall.

"You're acting weird, Sakuta."

"I am?"

"Usually, you'd be all, 'That's not true.' Or 'Then don't eat 'em!' "

"Yeah?"

"Yeah."

"I think most people get happy when someone compliments their girlfriend."

"I guess that makes sense. Still…"

"Still, what?"

"You aren't most people."

As he answered, Sakuta was putting the lunch box together, stacking the two layers, then the lid, then putting a rubber band around the whole thing. He wrapped it and a chopsticks case in a napkin and took it back to the table.

Kaede had sped up at last and was putting the last bite of wiener in her mouth. As she chewed away, he dropped the napkin-wrapped lunch box in front of her.

"Don't forget this."

She looked it over.

Then she swallowed and asked, "What is it?"

"What does it look like?"

"Lunch."

"Correct."

"Didn't I say I'd just buy some *onigiri* at a store?"

"If you don't want it, I'll eat it."

He reached out for it, but Kaede's hands shot out first, pulling it toward her and hugging it tight.

"I want it."

"Don't shake it up too much, or the food'll mix together."

"……"

She gingerly put it back on the table. Then she looked up at him.

"U-um, Sakuta…"

"Don't yell at me if it tastes like ass."

"I—I totally will! But that's not the point."

She shot him a glare for forcing a tangent.

"…Thanks for the lunch. I'm glad you made it."

"You're welcome."

He cleared the rest of the table.

"I can clear my own!" Kaede said, too late.

"You wanted to get going early, right? Better go change."

You had to account for delayed trains and whatever else. Plus, Kaede was supersensitive to unwanted attention, so it couldn't hurt to get there ahead of the crowds. Hence the early departure.

So Sakuta took over the cleanup, carrying the dishes to the sink. As he did, Kaede thanked him again.

"We'll meet up in the living room once you're changed."

"Okay!" she said, and she headed to her room.

When he was done washing the dishes, Sakuta went to his own room and changed into his uniform. When he got back to the living room, their cat, Nasuno, was coming out from the half-open door to Kaede's room, so he put some food in her bowl. She meowed at him once and then started munching away.

Kaede emerged right as Nasuno emptied the bowl.

She had her coat on over her junior high uniform, scarf and mittens, thick black tights—ready for the cold. Her outfit might be warm, but as she put her backpack on, her cheeks were stiffening up. That much was unavoidable. If telling people not to worry actually eased stress, nobody would ever be stressed in the first place. So Sakuta paid it no heed, focusing on other things.

"Got your admission slip?"

"Mm."

Very small nod.

"The lunch in there?"

"It is."

Bigger nod.

"Pencil box?"

"Ready to go."

"You've got everything?"

"Yeah…," she said, then let out a squeak and ran back in her room without saying why. The door slammed so hard Nasuno jumped.

He could hear her footsteps running back and forth inside.

"What do you make of it?" Sakuta asked, but Nasuno didn't answer. Instead, Kaede's door opened, and she came out.

She didn't look any different. She maybe had a tighter grip on the straps of her backpack. She still looked tense, but there was a note of steel in her eyes.

"Now I'm good!"

He had no clue what was good, but she seemed more prepared, so he decided not to pry.

"Get too fired up now, you'll wear yourself out."

"I-I've got it under control."

"Then let's hit the road."

Peppering her with questions wasn't gonna help her relax. So Sakuta headed for the door.

He got his shoes on and waited for Kaede to do the same.

"……"

Kaede gave him a silent nod. Good to go. Sakuta looked down the hall, spotted Nasuno's face around the corner, and said, "Guard the fort."

They stepped outside, he locked the door, and they took the elevator nonstop to ground level.

Outside there was a chill in the air, and their breaths formed clouds in front of them.

Kaede was definitely walking slower than he was, so he matched her pace. They headed for Fujisawa Station. On the way, they caught a red light and had to wait for it to change. They reached the main road and crossed the bridge over the Sakai River.

The whole time, Kaede didn't say a word. Neither did Sakuta. She looked like she was thinking hard. Probably reviewing everything she'd studied one last time. Seemed stupid to interrupt.

If her head was full of test stuff, that could only be a good thing. If she was focused, then she'd spend less time worrying about anyone looking at her, and they could avoid her Adolescence Syndrome flaring up again.

And if she could safely get through the exam itself, that would give her more confidence. And the more confidence she built, the less worried she'd be about the attention and opinions of strangers.

Right now she had a fragment of courage not yet converted to confidence. This was just the first step.

She was scared, but she was working hard. She'd made up her mind to do so.

"...What, Sakuta?" she asked, catching him looking at her.

"Nothing," he said, but she clearly wanted more, so he added, "That's a nice scarf."

"Mai gave it to me. It's very warm."

She seemed pretty proud of that.

"That's my Mai."

"You always say that."

For some reason, she sounded rather annoyed.

On his own, this walk usually took Sakuta ten minutes, but it took twice that today. Sakuta and Kaede reached the station after a full twenty-minute walk. They went up the stairs by the electronics shop one at a time and reached the elevated walkway.

Since they'd left early, the station was mostly filled with suits on their way to work. There were uniformed students, but far fewer than when Sakuta usually passed through.

But the building that housed the Odakyu Enoshima Line and the JR station was, as always, absolutely jam-packed. If he wasn't careful, he and Kaede could easily get separated.

Well aware of the risk, Kaede stuck to his back like glue, without him needing to say a word. They pushed through the congestion to the south end of the station.

Across the connective bridge was a department store. At the entrance, they turned right and saw the Enoden Fujisawa Station up ahead.

They paused at the ticket machines.

Kaede went to buy her own ticket. She put money in, pressed the button, and came back with the ticket in hand, looking proud of herself.

"I'll have you know, I can *also* buy tickets."

"I know that!"

Obviously not the response she'd wanted. Kaede pursed her lips at him.

They moved toward the gates a few yards away.

"Don't get off at the wrong station."

"I already went to Shichirigahama to deliver the application. I'll be fine."

Kaede buried her cheeks in her scarf, clearly not wanting him to baby her further.

"Well, we did everything we could, so go do everything you can."

"Mm."

This was as far as he could go. She'd have to make it all the way to the testing center at Minegahara on her own, take the test alone, and come back flying solo.

They'd talked about it a few days earlier and decided as much.

Sakuta had been planning on going all the way to school with her, explaining her history to them, and hanging out in an empty class until she was done, but Kaede had insisted she wanted to do things the way everyone else did.

He'd talked with Miwako, and they'd decided to respect her wishes. The whole goal here was to attend a conventional school. If she passed and got into Minegahara, she'd spend the bulk of the next three years going to school, often alone. It would be routine. It wasn't *just* today.

"Talk to a teacher if anything goes wrong."

"Mm."

"Okay."

"Oh, wait…Sakuta."

He'd turned to go, but she called out, stopping him.

"Mm?"

"……"

She clearly had something to say, but nothing came out. She just gripped her backpack strap even tighter.

"Better get it off your chest, whatever it is. You don't wanna be thinking about it during the exam. And if you do get distracted by whatever this is, I don't want you blaming me."

"I wouldn't do that."

"Then let's hear it."

"Er, um." Kaede hung her head, really struggling to say what was on her mind.

"Yeah?"

"I can work hard, too."

"Don't push yourself."

"I'm being serious."

"Seriously, you're already working plenty hard."

"But I can work harder, too."

She caught his eye for emphasis. Behind her, the green-and-cream retro car was pulling into the station.

Kaede heard it and looked over her shoulder.

"Train's here."

"I know! Thanks for walking me here."

Kaede waved, ran her ticket through the gate, and stepped inside. She glanced back once, making sure he was still watching, smiled sheepishly, and then darted toward the train.

She got at the back of the line and safely made it on board.

Sakuta watched until the train pulled out, and then he left the gates.

He headed back the way he'd come, through the Odakyu/JR building, and out the north side. Across the pedestrian overpass, thinking about Kaede's words.

——*"I can work hard, too."*

That *too* stuck with him. Who did she mean by it?

There were lots of people out there working hard.

Kaede was hardly the only exam student doing as much.

Sakuta himself was working hard, prepping for his college exams next year.

Mai was working hard at being famous, Nodoka was working hard at the whole idol thing. People all around the world, working on one thing or another.

But Kaede's *too* wasn't talking about any of them. There was only one person she could mean by that.

Someone always on her mind.

Someone she'd never met but would never forget.

The other Kaede.

"Can't exactly tell her not to let it bug her, can I?"

2

Once Sakuta returned home from walking Kaede to the station, he changed back into indoor clothes. Since the classrooms were being used for exams, he had no school today.

He carried his dirty socks to the washroom and dropped them into the laundry machine outside the bath. He dumped everything in the basket in after them and started the cycle.

For a while, he watched the clothing spin, but then he got bored and pulled out the vacuum cleaner.

He went around the living room, dining area, kitchen, entrance, and both bedrooms, sucking up all the dust. Just as he finished, the laundry machine beeped, calling to him.

"I'm coming," he said.

He put the vacuum cleaner away and went back to the washroom. The spin-dry cycle was done, and he took each article out one at a time, hanging them up. Sakuta's shirt and underwear, Kaede's pajamas and underthings.

He felt like she'd once sworn she was gonna wash her own underwear, but that had yet to actually bear fruit.

A few underthings made no real difference to Sakuta's workload, so he didn't *really* care.

Once it was all hung up, he took Nasuno to his room. He turned on the heater and sat down at his desk. Since he'd woken up early, he was craving a nap, but Kaede was out there slaving over her exam, and he figured he'd better get some studying done.

He opened a book of math problems. One designed for college exam prep. He worked out the answer to a problem involving quadratic functions and wrote it down in his notebook.

There were six or seven similar books on his desk. Math, physics, and English. All of these had been added two weeks ago, and none of them by Sakuta himself. Mai was bringing them over, a new one each time she came to help Kaede study.

Half were new, half were hand-me-downs, books she'd used herself. She'd shown no outward signs of studying at all, but these books were pretty well worked over. And since she'd handed them over with a smile, saying, "This'll help you a lot!" he had to take them.

His bedroom was slowly but steadily getting an exam-student remodel. Contractor: Mai.

He felt like failing was long since not an option. But Mai seemed to be enjoying herself, so it was just a matter of doing his part. If that didn't work, Mai would forgive him. Probably.

He solved another math problem. This one was a trigonometric function. Stuff he'd covered in his first year.

Since he and Mai started dating, she'd often helped him study for tests, so he wasn't really struggling that much with the Center Test material. But the tougher problems on his target school's general and secondary entrance exams were completely defeating him.

Specifically, both math and physics problems were a jumble of things from several different fields. If he couldn't dig down to what the problem actually was, he had no idea how to even begin tackling it, and even if he got an answer, he often found he'd been solving something entirely wrong. He was starting to see why most people started studying in summer.

He spent a good two hours wrestling with these complexities.

Sakuta's focus was interrupted by a growl from his stomach. He was hungrier than he'd realized. He looked up at the clock; it was just past noon.

"Time to eat."

He'd been talking to himself but got an actual answer—Nasuno had been curled up on his bed, but she looked up and meowed at him.

He left his notebook open on his desk and stood up. Nasuno followed him out.

Sakuta fed Nasuno first, then opened the fridge to get his own food ready. He pulled out the leftover ground meat mix.

He formed a large patty, put a depression in the center, and dropped it on the pan. Got both sides seared, then lowered the flame. While he waited for that to cook through, he used the rest of the rice from that morning to make a big heap on a round plate. He put the rest of the potato salad next to it, and the fully cooked Salisbury steak next to that. Did this count as Hawaiian style? Who knew.

No part of the living room felt like a tropical getaway. He sat down at the *kotatsu*, switched it on, and began eating. The patty was cooked and seasoned well. Kaede would be pleased.

Halfway through the meal, he turned the TV on. There was a news and talk show airing.

They were running a segment where comedians and models ran from one popular sweet shop after another, trying to see who could get the most specialties before they were sold out. Laughs and tears.

Sakuta watched dispassionately, munching on his meal. They cut to a commercial before anyone reached the next destination.

"Oh!" he said—because he knew the face on his screen.

It was Mai.

She was in a snow-covered landscape, on the platform of some train station, sitting alone with a red scarf on.

This must've been the commercial she'd filmed in Nagasaki last month. It had snowed heavily in Kyushu, and she said they'd rushed down to get filming done.

She looked sad, like she was waiting for someone. There was no dialogue. Just her white breath in the air, her eyes downcast as she ate a piece of chocolate. The narration revealed this was for a wintertime-limited chocolate said to melt in your mouth like snowflakes. Fifteen seconds into the spot, Mai heard someone coming and looked toward the camera. And smiled.

That look was certainly the capper on the ad. It would never have worked with any actress but her.

"See? My Mai's the cutest."

But today of all days, seeing Mai in a commercial like this kinda stung.

It was February 16.

Two days ago had been the fourteenth—Valentine's Day.

But for three days now they'd been unable to meet up. He hadn't even heard her voice.

She'd headed out on the thirteenth for a location shoot in Kyoto. And they were keeping her too busy to even call.

He shot a baleful glare at the landline phone. And lo and behold, it rang.

"The hand of fate!"

Even better if it turned out to be Mai. Heart leaping, he scrambled out from under the *kotatsu*. Picking up the remote, he lowered the volume, then checked the phone's display. The ten digits shown were his favorites—Mai's cell phone number.

It *was* her.

He snatched up the receiver and put it to his ear.

"Tell me, Mai," he said, immediately disgruntled.

"What?" she asked, on guard.

This was obviously not how she'd expected him to answer. He didn't care.

"Have you ever heard of Valentine's Day?" he asked.

"Who hasn't?" she scoffed.

"I just thought you might not have."

"Well, I have!" she insisted.

"Then when is it?"

"February fourteenth."

"So what do people do that day?"

"I'm guessing you wanted to get chocolate from me and then do something even sweeter together."

"Specifically, I was thinking of you in a bunny-girl costume with my head on your lap, feeding me chocolate."

"You'd choke on it," she laughed. "More importantly, how's Kaede holding up?"

Completely brushing off his disappointment *and* changing the subject. But that was clearly why she was calling.

"Can't we talk about me a little longer?"

"You made her the scrambled eggs?"

Sadly, his request gained no traction. Didn't even warrant attention.

"I did," he said, pushing aside the temptation to sulk. "She looked really happy about them."

Mai had taught him how to make those scrambled eggs, so he was honor bound to report the outcome.

"Okay. Good."

"Kaede set out all fired up. I got out of bed early to make her lunch, and she's probably eating it now."

His heart was not entirely in this conversation. He glanced at the TV, and the clock on the screen showed exactly one PM.

"The exam covers English, Japanese, and math in the morning?"

"Right."

The afternoon was social studies and science. Then they held interviews until the eighteenth. Kaede's interview wasn't until the last day, so she'd be coming home after two more hours of testing.

"Should wrap up around three, then?"

"I guess."

And she'd be home by four.

"You're worried?"

"Won't make her scores any better."

"What were you up to?"

"Studying. Angling to get some approval from you."

"Fine, I approve," she said, like she was shooing away a toddler.

"No rewards?"

"Should I come visit with a ribbon round my neck? Apologize for missing Valentine's Day?"

She was answering his pleas with *jokes*.

"That sounds perfect!" he said.

"Well, *after* the exams."

"Kaede's?"

Those would be done first. Today, really. The quickest route!

"Nooope."

Naturally, Mai was having none of it.

"So definitely mine?"

That was at least a year off. Too far to look forward to. And it turned the screws up on the pressure to pass, which got an audible sigh out of him.

"Can you wait that long, Sakuta?" Mai asked. There was a wink in her voice.

"Mm?"

She was taking this a different direction and momentarily lost him.

"This'll be after *my* exams," she clarified. Her voice had grown a bit softer. Maybe a hint of embarrassment.

"Really?"

"Does that not do it for you?"

It totally did. Just…

"I was all assuming you wouldn't let me lay a finger on you until I got into college."

"If I said that, I wouldn't be able to lay a finger on *you*, either."

"Mai, are you getting urges?"

"I didn't mean it sexually."

He'd been teasing, but her tone was super normal, which in turn seemed off. Usually, when he said things like that, Mai would start making threats, like "Fine, then nothing until you've officially passed!" and took delight in making him plea for mercy.

"Mai, are you having a rough time?"

"Where'd that come from? No. Filming's going great."

This sounded totally natural, not a hint of anything wrong. But…this was Mai Sakurajima. She could do that. She'd been "acting natural" her whole damn life.

So Sakuta said, "Should I come up and give you a hug?"

"Ryouko would be livid. Better not."

She brushed aside his offer with a joke. Her tone was very bright. No hint of darkness. Like she was deeply enjoying their conversation. This was the Mai he loved the most.

"You wait right there for Kaede to get home. Her test won't end until she's safely back with you."

As he searched for a response, Mai said, "Oh, sorry, Ryouko's calling. I gotta go."

"Mai—thanks."

"Mm?"

"It's been a long three days."

"I promise if I'm on a location shoot, I'll find time to call every day from now on. And I'll be back tomorrow. Bye."

And with that tender note, she hung up. All traces of her vanished in an instant.

There was no point holding the phone any longer, so he put it back on the cradle.

"What part of Kyoto is she in…?" he wondered.

If he left now, what would be the fastest route to get to her? He had a feeling taking the Shinkansen from Shin-Yokohama would be faster than going through Odawara.

But even as he thought about it, the phone rang again.

"Did Mai forget something?"

He checked the number as he reached for the receiver, but it wasn't Mai's cell. He knew the area code, but not the number itself.

Which was enough to tell him this was bad news.

"Azusagawa," he said, as calmly as he could manage.

"Er, I'm a faculty member at Minegahara High School."

Sakuta recognized the man's voice—it was his own homeroom teacher.

"It's me," he said. "Sakuta."

"Oh, I see."

The man's tone got a tad less formal. But no less tense. The moment the phone rang, Sakuta had known why.

"Something happen with Kaede? My sister?"

He had talked with them about her issues. Explained that after a long time out of school, she might break down during the test.

"Yeah. She started feeling unwell during the lunch break."

"……"

"She's resting in the nurse's office but doesn't seem to want to talk to anyone."

It wasn't like he'd been unprepared for the possibility. Sakuta had known this might happen. But he'd really hoped it wouldn't, and Kaede had been working so hard, he'd started to think she might actually manage to get through this.

So the news definitely hit him pretty hard.

But this was no time to wallow in depression.

"Azusagawa, can you get here?"

"I'm on my way."

By the time he spoke, he was calm again.

"We should also let your parents know—"

"I'll tell them."

"Okay, then. We'll be here."

The call disconnected, leaving Sakuta with the phone buzzing in his ear. He quickly dialed his dad's cell phone number. It rang a few times, then went to voice mail.

"The school called. Kaede fell apart during lunch. I'm on my way there. I'll call again."

He kept it short and to the point and hung up.

Half his lunch was still sitting there, so he quickly choked it down, then changed and grabbed his jacket on the way out the door.

3

This morning he and Kaede had taken twenty minutes to reach Fujisawa Station, but now he made it in five.

He ran up to the Enoden Fujisawa Station, panting heavily, and saw a Kamakura-bound train on the platform. He ran his train pass through the gate and jumped on the nearest car even as the departure bells rang.

The doors closed on his heels.

The train slowly pulled out and rolled slowly down the tracks before stopping at the next station, Ishigami. A few people got out, and it rolled leisurely away.

If he wasn't in such a hurry, this speed would never have bothered him. Normally, the way these retro cars rattled along the coast town roads was a lovely seasoning on a commute that could easily have been a dull routine.

Right now, he just wanted to be at school already, and it was driving him nuts. But by the time they reached the next station, his panic had subsided.

The laughter of the tourists, the lived-in vibe of the locals, and the relaxed pace of the train itself all helped. Sakuta realized *he* was the one out of line.

Feeling like all those things were telling him to chill out, Sakuta plunked himself down on an empty seat.

Fretting would do him *no* good now. He couldn't make the train go faster. The best thing he could do for Kaede now was to get a grip.

There was no guarantee their father could get away, so Sakuta might well be the only person there for her.

He wiped the sweat from his brow and caught his breath again. He inhaled all the way and slowly let it out. He repeated that until the urgency that had lent wings to his feet died away.

The train kept rolling another fifteen minutes and dropped Sakuta at Shichirigahama exactly when the timetable said it would.

*   *   *

Minegahara was a short walk from the station, and he took it at a brisk pace, then headed to the visitors' entrance. For the simple reason that it was closer to the nurse's office than the normal student entrance.

He grabbed a pair of visitor slippers and just ditched his shoes there before stepping inside. The exams were still ongoing, and there was an eerie hush in the halls. He could tell there were plenty of people around, yet none of them were making noise. Like the chilly winter air, their stifled stress pricked his skin.

Shaking that off, he took big strides down the hall, slippers flapping.

The teacher who'd called him was waiting outside the door. He saw Sakuta coming and looked grave.

"That was quick, Azusagawa."

"I ran," he said, as if that was the natural thing to do. "Is she...?"

"She's resting inside, but..."

He glanced at the door, keeping his words terse. Nothing specific about her condition. And the look on his face showed he was rattled.

"It's a lot to handle, I know," Sakuta said, bowing his head.

"No, you warned us in advance. Wish we could have done more."

"Thanks for letting me know."

And with that, he opened the door, trying not to make too much noise.

The nurse was sitting at the desk inside, her back to him. She spun her seat as Sakuta closed the door.

Their eyes met, he bowed, and she pointed silently at the partitioned-off bed. Kaede was resting there.

Sakuta slipped through the curtains and sat down on the stool by the bed.

No part of Kaede was visible here. Just a heap of covers.

"Kaede," he said, and the heap twitched. Looked like she wasn't asleep. "I'm here. Care to pop your face out?"

"......"

No answer. Didn't even move.

"Any pain?"

"……"

Still no response.

She'd probably been like this for a while before he came. Which explained his teacher's consternation and why the nurse was just watching over her at a respectful distance. Being with anyone was hard for Kaede right now.

"They said you got sick during lunch."

"……"

"It wasn't the lunch I made, was it? If so, sorry."

He'd figured she still wouldn't answer.

But a raspy whisper emerged from the pile of covers.

"…It was really good."

"So good it threw you off your game?"

"…No."

A bit more emotion behind that.

"……I left early, so…"

"Mm."

"I got here before the crowds."

"Okay."

"But there were already two students in the classroom."

"Third place is a solid result. Bronze medal."

Kaede didn't laugh.

"At first, I was too scared to go in, but when I did, nobody looked at me. So I made it to my seat."

"Leaving early was the right choice, then."

"Mm. Lots more people came in, but everyone was focused on last-minute reviewing. Nobody cared about me."

"Everyone's stressing about the test."

Pass or fail. A fork in their paths. Messing this up meant no clear road ahead, a future shrouded in darkness. A critical juncture for anyone their age.

"When the bell rang, they explained the rules. The first test was English, and it went really well."

Her tone was brightening a little.

"Great."

"One of the things Nodoka taught me was on it, and I thought, 'Yes!'"

"Toyohama's really gunning for that idol-with-a-higher-education thing."

She might be styled like a razzle-dazzle blond, but she was actually really smart.

"Second-period Japanese had stuff about similar-looking kanji that Mai taught me, so I knew exactly which ones to use."

"That's my Mai, all right."

"And third-period math had factorization problems like you showed me."

"And you solved them?"

"I did."

"Well, you worked hard to learn that."

They hadn't had that much time between the decision to apply and the exam itself. Barely a month. But Kaede had crammed all the studying she could into that space, staying up so late she fell asleep at her desk any number of times.

"You, Mai, and Nodoka all made it so the morning tests went well."

"Good."

"I was doing *so* well…"

Her voice grew choked with tears. Half of it went through her nose, and her voice broke.

"And the lunch was great. I thought I could get through the afternoon, too."

She clenched her teeth, her voice shaking.

"Mm-hmm."

"But then…then…"

"……Mm."

"I'm a mess. I can't do anything!"

Her voice echoed in the silence of the nurse's office.

"You totally can. You got all the morning tests right."

"…There was a girl with the same uniform."

"……"

"I went to the bathroom, and in the hall…our eyes met."

"Same uniform" must have meant the uniform from Kaede's junior high. The place she'd only *just* managed to start attending, if only in the nurse's office. They were both from the same school but had been taking exams in different rooms because Kaede had chosen an off day to turn in her application. She hadn't come with the rest of the students from her school. And as a result, she'd been seated away from the others.

"The moment I thought she was looking at me, I got scared. Felt sick. My hands, legs, stomach, everything hurt. The bruises showed up. I couldn't move. I had to go back and take the test, but…"

She was sniffling, her body quivering.

"I wanted to work hard. Go back to the classroom and sit like everyone else. I knew I had to, but my chest got all tight…and I was too scared. I'd been fine a moment before, but the fear just wouldn't go away."

She was crying in the darkness beneath the covers, shaking.

"Kaede, you worked very hard."

"I didn't!"

She was crying even harder now.

"You did. That's why it hurts so bad."

"!"

The entire pile jumped at that, but then she whispered "I didn't" again. Barely voiced. "I didn't work hard. I couldn't do anything."

She just kept looping that thought.

"I'm a mess. I can't work hard. I wanted to, but I just… I can't."

"You worked crazy hard. Trust me, I was there."

He meant every word of that. Frankly, he thought she'd worked a bit too hard. But nothing he said was getting through.

"The other Kaede worked *much* harder!"

This was almost a shriek, and it shook the room. That was enough to get the nurse to poke her head through the curtains. "Don't worry," Sakuta said. She nodded and went back to her desk.

".......,"

".......,"

Their respective silences hung in the air.

He hadn't noticed the whir of the heater before, but now it seemed deafening.

He looked for words, but nothing seemed right.

——*"The other Kaede worked* much *harder!"*

There weren't many words that could match the strength of the sorrow behind that.

Kaede spoke first.

"All this is because she was there."

"The work you've done is *yours*, Kaede."

That much was true.

"Mai and Nodoka are only nice to me because they know how hard the other Kaede worked."

Still sobbing, still buried in blankets, Kaede kept on wailing.

"She gave me *everything*. She gave me all these lovely people. But I can't...I can't do *anything*."

Her heart was sinking deeper and deeper into a mire of sadness.

"Everyone helped me study. Mai, Nodoka, you...and I can't give you anything back. I can't give *her* anything back."

And that sadness kept her crying.

"Nobody's expecting anything back."

That hadn't been why they'd supported her. Frankly, Sakuta had never once been convinced Kaede even *should* go to Minegahara. It was hardly the only right choice she had.

He wanted something more important. Something more fundamental.

Sakuta wanted Kaede to be happy. To live a happy life. That's all.

A life of perfectly decent days spent laughing about nothing. That was the kind of happy he aspired to.

"But I know better!"

He couldn't seem to convince Kaede of this. This idea of giving back was all that mattered to her, and since he cared about her, he'd helped her do things her way.

"I know she was better than me," Kaede whispered. "I should have stayed her."

As the meaning of that sank in, a wave of shock and panic washed over him. And he knew that feeling was caused by his own frustrations.

"Listen, Kaede...," he began, a hint of irritation seeping into his voice. Not with her. With the fact that she was in a position to be talking like this at all.

"You liked the other Kaede better!"

"!"

A hot geyser of emotions he could not put in words forced him up off the stool and onto his feet. A vehement storm raging within, a whirl of fire. Before he could breathe any of that out—

"Azusagawa, got a sec?"

He was interrupted by a voice through the curtains. His homeroom teacher.

"......"

The timing was so horrendous he just glared at the man.

"Can it wait?"

The man flinched, but that helped cool Sakuta's head.

"...No, it's fine. What is it?"

"The exam ended, and the classroom emptied. Your sister's things are still there."

Sakuta looked back at Kaede.

"......"

She still had the covers on.

If they kept talking while this riled up, he felt their emotions would just get in the way. So he looked at his teacher and said, "Fine."

He turned to Kaede, said, "I'll be right back," and left without waiting for an answer.

The teacher took him to room 2-1.

Sakuta's own classroom. Kaede had been taking her test here.

She hadn't been at Sakuta's desk, but it was weird to think of her sitting where he always did.

"Can you take it from here? I've got a lot on my plate."

The man had the grace to look apologetic.

"Yeah. And thanks."

"Call me if you need anything."

Sakuta nodded. The teacher nodded back and left the room.

Leaving Sakuta on his own.

He moved past the podium to the window. The fourth seat in that row alone still had a pencil sheet, exam ticket, and backpack.

From this seat, you could see the whole Shichirigahama beach. The sun was on its way westward, and the vibe was now rather forlorn, but the weather had been great that morning, and it must have been a spectacular sight.

"Wonder if she even had it in her to notice."

He figured she'd probably kept her eyes down until she found her desk. And once seated, she put out her ticket and pencil box and then kept her head down again, making sure she didn't meet anyone else's eyes.

That seemed like a real shame.

Shaking his head, Sakuta put her ticket and pencil box in her backpack. As he did, his fingers brushed against a thick notebook.

"Is this…?"

He knew what it was. He'd been the one who bought it, after all. It was the notebook he'd given the other Kaede. It had her name on the cover in hiragana.

The diary she'd spent two years filling.

"She brought it with her?"

It had nothing to do with the exam. Flipping through it wouldn't give her any last-minute test-taking tips.

But she'd put the other Kaede's notebook in her bag and brought it with her.

He found himself reaching for it.

Sakuta took it out of the backpack and flipped through it.

It fell open on one page—a page she must have opened to a lot.

It was written in the other Kaede's handwriting. She always wrote each letter so carefully. You could tell how earnestly she meant each word.

Sakuta's eyes were drawn to a line on this page.

I want to go to the same school as Sakuta. That's one of my dreams.

The moment he read that, heat shot through him, rising up behind his nose and burning behind his eyes.

If he hadn't snapped his head up and held them in, he'd have let tears fall on the page.

"That's...right."

He forced the words out, but they still sounded choked with tears.

Part of him had known. Or at least imagined this was why. But seeing it written out like this in *her* handwriting really hit hard.

Of course. *This* was why Kaede had been so fixated on coming here. It was what the other Kaede had wanted.

Kaede knew how hard her other self had worked. While she'd taken a two-year rest, the other Kaede had done her best to live. And this was a dream she'd been unable to make true herself.

She'd said she wanted to apply at Minegahara in the hopes that doing so would pay the other Kaede back for everything she'd done.

She'd spent day after day working hard to pass this test.

And then she'd fallen apart at lunch. Been so down on herself. Said *that* to him.

——*"You liked the other Kaede better!"*

He took several deep breaths until the rush behind his eyes faded. Then he closed the other Kaede's notebook and put it in the bag.

He picked up Kaede's coat and left the classroom.

Down the hall and down the stairs.

He turned toward the nurse's office but kept going past the door.

This brought him to the main office. There was a pay phone just hanging out in the hall here, and he picked up the receiver.

Dropped in a few ten-yen coins.

"……"

Punched in ten digits.

One of the more recent additions to his mental phone directory.

It rang three times, then she picked up.

"Hello…?"

A girl's voice, guarded.

"Toyohama? It's me. Azusagawa."

"I should have known."

"I'm literally the only person in the world who uses pay phones."

"What do you want?"

She got right down to business.

"Got a favor to ask."

So he did, too.

"……?"

Her breath sounded surprised, but she said nothing.

"You're the only person I can ask."

She must have caught something in his tone.

"So what do you need?" she asked.

4

The Minegahara school building was reserved for testing from February 16 through the eighteenth, so when classes did resume, everyone had graduation on their minds.

Private university testing wrapped up around the same time as the high school exams. Some third-year students were already free of that cycle, and the day after classes resumed— February 20—the rooms were starting to fill with giddy laughs.

A far cry from the crackling tension of the weeks prior.

Sensing that change in the air, Sakuta headed for the library in lieu of eating lunch.

Not because he had anything he wanted to read or any books to borrow. There was only one reason he'd brave the chilly hallways to the library.

He'd promised Mai he would.

He slid open the library doors.

It felt like the library's hush spilled out into the hall behind him.

Sakuta stepped forward into the room. He closed the door behind him and advanced through the deserted library interior.

The space was well heated. He walked through rows of bookshelves, each taller than him.

When he emerged from their shadows, he found a single soul, seated by the windows.

She sat with her back to him, bolt upright.

Long black hair.

Mai.

She didn't seem aware of his approach.

That puzzled him, but as he got closer, he realized she had earbuds in. A set of exam study problems and a notebook were open in front of her, but her attention was entirely on her phone's screen.

She must have been very focused. He sneaked up behind her, but she still didn't notice. Figuring this was his chance, he reached out and put his arms around her, hugging her tight.

"……"

He'd been trying to surprise her, but she didn't yelp or even jump. He could tell she hadn't even gone tense. Apparently, she *had* known he was there.

That was disappointing, but a sweet scent tickled his nostrils.

"You smell really good, Mai."

And that made him feel a lot better.

"Don't *smell* people," she said, laughing. And flicked his forehead.

"Ow."

"It didn't hurt."

She giggled again. She was still in his arms and not objecting to that. He'd assumed she'd be telling him to let go by now.

"......"

"......"

Accepting his embrace, sinking into it, Mai never let her eyes leave her phone.

And that made him worried, so he asked.

"Mai."

"What?"

"Is it okay if I keep hugging you?"

"Why not? It's winter."

She was just *encouraging* him.

"Winter's the best."

Could it stay winter forever?

"Just don't get carried away and start grabbing anything weird."

"No part of you could possibly be weird."

He started sliding one hand toward her chest.

"Are you looking to end this now?"

"I swear, nothing about you is weird!"

"......"

The silent pressure proved intimidating, and he put his hand back where it was. Shoulders were safe. He was basking in the smell of her shampoo. He could feel the heat of her body, feel the beating of her heart. There was something deeply comforting about being this close to someone you loved.

"Whatcha watchin', Mai?"

He was looking over her shoulder at the phone in her hand. There was a video playing on it with plenty of CGI, but he couldn't quite figure out what it was.

Mai took one earbud out and handed it to him. He popped it in his left ear and heard a woman's voice purring over some jaunty tunes.

"She's building a fan base through social media, mostly big with students. A girl from my agency told me about her when we were on a shoot together."

She turned the phone so he could see better. The visuals were kinda mystic, dreamlike, shifting to match the music. The song told a story, starting soft, growing emotional, until the singer finally poured her whole heart out. This seemed to be a self-made music video.

He felt like he'd heard this before somewhere but couldn't place it. If it was popular with students, he'd probably heard it in passing somewhere. On breaks at school, at work, or on the train.

Every now and then it showed a glimpse of someone singing, but the face was obscured, and he couldn't make it out. But he got the feeling she was their age.

"Nobody knows who she is or what she looks like. That's part of the appeal."

The video was uploaded by Touko Kirishima. That struck him as a pretty name. But if she was hiding her face, then it seemed likely that was just a stage name…

The song was as effervescent as the name, like a fable set to melody.

But the emotions in it were very modern social ones—love, friendship, loneliness, and kindness.

He could tell why her work appealed to teenagers. There was a raw vein of anxiety and discontent behind it, and these emotions sprang from that.

As the song wound on, both Sakuta and Mai fell silent, listening until the end. It lasted five full minutes.

The screen showed the first shot of the video, with a prompt to repeat, but Mai took her earbud out and turned the screen off.

"What did you think of it, Mai?"

"The visuals are rich, and the song itself pleasant. It'll give me something to discuss with the girl who recommended it."

That sounded like her real motivation for listening to this song. She pulled a bit of a face as she said it. Celebrity socializing was a burden in its own right.

"More importantly, Sakuta."

"Mm?"

"Time you let go."

"Aww."

"I'm getting hot."

"But it's winter!"

"And I can't see your face."

She certainly had him wrapped around her finger.

"Well, if you put it that way," he said, letting go.

He stood up and moved to the seat across from her.

"I didn't know you liked my face that much."

"It's certainly never dull."

Not the compliment he'd been fishing for.

"They say you get tired of beauty after three days, but that's obviously a lie."

"How so?" Mai asked, clearly well aware of what he meant but relishing it anyway.

"I mean, I've yet to get tired of *your* beauty."

His answer seemed to satisfy her, and she smiled. Definitely a touch of glee there.

But then she remembered, and she put the smile away.

"How's Kaede holding up?"

"Depressed."

"Well, yeah…"

Four days ago, she'd come to their school to take her exams. But since that disaster, she hadn't once set foot outside, let alone made it to the nurse's office at her junior high. She was back to her home-alone self.

"She worked so hard, too," Mai whispered.

Kaede really had. All that studying, all the fears she'd pushed aside to make it to the exam center…even if she hadn't managed to take the afternoon tests, she had plenty to be proud about.

But all she could think was *The other me worked harder.*

She kept comparing herself negatively with the other Kaede.

That Kaede had dreamed about going to Minegahara High, and this Kaede felt guilty for not making that happen. Sakuta, Mai, and Nodoka had all helped her study, and she felt like she'd let them all down.

Even though not one of them—the other Kaede included—would ever dream of putting her down.

"She's gonna have to pull herself through," Sakuta said.

"Mm." Mai nodded.

Then the warning bell rang. Five minutes before break ended.

"I'm afraid that's all for today's date."

"We've still got five minutes!"

Mai dismissed that with a smirk as she put her notebook away. She stood up and put her coat on, too.

"......"

Sakuta stayed seated, looking up at her.

"I'm going home," she said, clearly done indulging him.

He gave up and got to his feet.

"I've got more exams next week. Anything you want to say to me?" she asked.

"Give it your best shot!" he said. This was his best effort to seem sincere.

And his reward was a look only he ever got to see. Slightly sheepish, mostly pleased, definitely happy.

With Mai gone, Sakuta had nothing better to do than roll back into room 2-1. He managed to mostly pay attention during the remaining classes.

After school, he went to work, teased Tomoe a bunch, and clocked out at nine.

And got home half an hour later.

"I'm back," he called, opening the door.

He took off his shoes and headed down the hall.

The light was on in the living room, but no sign of Kaede. Nasuno was curled up on the *kotatsu*, and she briefly mewed at him.

Kaede's door was firmly closed.

But she hadn't been cooped up in there all day. There were signs she'd been out here on the *kotatsu* next to the cat.

At the end of the table was a stack of A4-size envelopes. All kinds of colors. Blue, yellow, green, and white. Each of them with pamphlets for different remote-learning schools.

Half of these were places Sakuta had secretly visited on weekends. The other half were places their father had found or Miwako had provided. There were fifteen in all.

Sakuta had left the stack where Kaede would see them, and they were piled in a different order from this morning.

She'd clearly found them.

He opened one and found evidence she'd looked at the contents, too.

He closed it and put it back on the stack, and the door behind him opened. Kaede was tentatively peering out through the crack in her door. Their eyes met.

"I'm home," he said.

Kaede's eyes dropped to the floor. But she managed a soft "W-welcome back, Sakuta."

And she opened the door more and came out.

"……"

She seemed like she had something to say, but not the courage to lift her head. She wound up just fidgeting awkwardly.

Sakuta waited patiently.

"So, um," Kaede began.

"Mm?"

"The other day…"

She was staring fixedly at the floor.

"Which day?"

"The exam day."

"Mm?"

"That thing I said to you…"

Looking even more rattled, she was restlessly rubbing her hands together in front of her.

Sakuta had a pretty good idea what she wanted to say. This wasn't the first time. They'd had similar interactions the day before, and the day before that.

About the exam day…

…and what she'd said to him.

That one accusation in particular.

But he didn't think it would help Kaede if he was the one who spelled it out. This seemed like something she had to come to grips with on her own. Not something *his* logic could settle.

"……"

"……"

He waited a while, but Kaede said nothing else. When she finally did open her mouth, she just muttered, "It's nothing," and her head sank even lower.

So he said, "Kaede," sounding just like always.

"Wh-what?"

She flinched. Her eyes looked up through her lashes, on guard.

"You got time tomorrow?"

"Huh?"

"No school on Saturday, so you're free, yeah?"

"Er, um. Yeah," she stammered, nodding like he'd expected.

"Then come out with me after lunch."

"Um."

"See you there!"

Slightly forced, but before she could object, he went into his room to change. She took a few steps after him…but didn't end up saying anything.

5

"Where are we *going*?"

They'd left Fujisawa Station on the Tokaido Line without Sakuta breathing a word about their destination.

He'd made fried rice for lunch, and after they'd finished eating it, as promised, the two of them had gone out together.

The sky out the east-facing window was as clear as he could have hoped, and the winter air made everything in the distance look pale.

"Tsujido," Sakuta said.

Only naming the station.

Kaede was hanging on to the pole by the door, and her eyes turned toward the simplified route map on the wall. If she started with Fujisawa, it wouldn't take her long to locate Tsujido.

"The next station?"

"As you can see!"

He pointed at the digital display, which was showing the next stop. "Tsujido."

And even as they spoke, the train swept them toward the station until the brakes kicked in and slowed them down. Kaede staggered and clung to the pole to support herself.

When the doors opened, they stepped out onto the platform.

They waited for the initial rush to die down a bit and then set out.

"So where are we *going*?"

Her voice came from behind him as they headed up the stairs.

"Like I said, Tsujido!"

"We're *at* Tsujido."

"Then our next stop is the north exit from the eastern gates."

Hard to tell which direction that actually was, but there were signs. Apparently, there were two actual gates, one east, one west. This station was certainly smaller than Fujisawa (which had three lines running through it) but didn't lack for foot traffic.

The buildings around it seemed to have been massively redeveloped recently, and they looked much more modern than anything around Fujisawa.

Outside the gates, they soon spotted the north exit. They had a simple choice of exiting to the south or the north, so it was hard to get wrong.

There were a *lot* of people coming and going, and the average age seemed pretty low. Groups of kids Sakuta's age and couples in college. And parents in their late twenties or early thirties with children in tow.

As they followed the flow of the crowd, Kaede's voice got a bit cross. "Sakuta, seriously, where are we going?"

He was probably pushing his luck by this point.

"We're here," he said, looking up.

Before them stood a huge shopping mall. Connected directly to the station via a covered deck, and the crowd flow went right from the gates on into the mall.

"Here?" Kaede said, looking puzzled.

They went inside.

"Well, somewhere in here," he said, grinding to a halt. He'd assumed they'd easily find what they were looking for, but that had been a huge mistake.

The mall itself just stretched forever, and it was impossible to tell where anything was. He looked around, found a map of the stores, and headed toward it.

But even then, there was too much information, and he was struggling to find their destination.

"……"

His eyes must have gone dead, because Kaede started looking worried.

"Sakuta?"

"Kaede, help me find the event stage."

"Huh?"

"You're my only hope!"

"Uh, okay…"

She was a little rattled, but with a job to do, Kaede began pouring over the map intently. A college couple passing behind them said, "This place is three times the size of the Tokyo Dome!" "Gosh, that's craaazy!"

"Hear that?" he said, assuming Kaede had been listening.

"Never been to Tokyo Dome, so that meant nothing," she said.

"Seriously. Japanese people should convert everything to the tatami scale."

"That would be a *lot* of tatami."

"Like a hundred thousand, you think?"

"…I can't imagine that, either."

"Really? It's just ten times ten thousand."

"Oh, the event stage."

Brushing off his crystal-clear explanation, Kaede held up the pamphlet she'd acquired while he wasn't looking. She pointed to the ground floor's outdoor area.

"Here."

It did say "event stage."

And the exit was right next to the entrance they'd used.

They went back the way they'd come and out to the stage. There were maybe three hundred people watching. Seventy percent male, 30 percent female, ranging from teenagers up to fortysomethings. All of them were there for the group onstage.

"It was a short show today, but thanks for coming!"

A girl speaking into a microphone, her voice echoing through the speakers. Three girls onstage, all in colorful clothes, like idol singers. Sakuta didn't know who they were, but they were probably *actually* idols.

The audience cheered and waved, and the girls ran offstage.

Once they were gone, the cheers gave way to a moment of silence.

"Here?" Kaede asked, looking baffled. Sakuta had stopped at the back of the venue. "But you have Mai."

These suspicions were unwarranted.

"You'll get it in a sec."

It wasn't his personal tastes that had brought him to an idol concert. He was here for the next person on, assuming they were still on schedule.

He looked to the stage, and the lady running things was introducing the next act.

"Sweet Bullet!" she cried, and seven idols ran out onto the stage.

"Oh!" Kaede said, her mouth dropping. "It's Nodoka!"

Surrounded by six brunettes, Nodoka and her blond locks sure popped. Kaede had been aware Nodoka was an idol but had never seen her perform. And Sakuta knew exactly why she looked so stunned. Until Sakuta had met Mai and Nodoka, part of him had never believed celebrities were real.

But here was the proof.

The seven members lined up in a row, calling out to the crowd together.

"We've got zilch for time, so let's hit our first song!"

The speaker was the long-haired girl in dead center, Uzuki Hirokawa.

Her honesty got a laugh.

And that was swallowed up by the intro. The number kicked off with a powerful solo from Uzuki herself, and Sweet Bullet's concert was underway.

The crowd were heating up. The front rows were waving glow sticks even though it was broad daylight.

And the routines onstage heated up, too, their formations shifting, their moves in perfect sync. A good mix of energy and grace that captivated the crowd. Even to an amateur eye, Uzuki Hirokawa stood out—always at the center, leading both songs and dances. He could tell Kaede's eyes were following her.

Nodoka was next in line and getting her share of attention. But Uzuki had something special. She just seemed so full of life. Her smile legitimately sparkled. He had no idea where she got her energy from, but it was certainly a force that drew people to her.

And the group finished the number off, going all out the whole time.

The music stopped, and the crowd roared. People were yelling "Zukki!" at Uzuki. The other members' nicknames soon joined them. Someone yelled out "Dokaaa!" for Nodoka. If no one else had stepped up, Sakuta had been getting ready to do that himself. Shame.

As the crowd roared, the Sweet Bullet members stealthily wiped their sweat and caught their breaths, smiling and waving.

They'd only done one number. And in the cold outdoor winter air. Yet even from this distance, he could see that their brows were glistening. That was just how big a workout that choreography had been.

Uzuki was straight up steaming. Spotting that, Nodoka said, "Zukki, your aura is palpable."

"Really? Then this must be a *good* day!"

The logic there wasn't clear, and Uzuki had taken the dig as a compliment and was blushing.

"We're all feeling it, right?" she asked, glancing around. "It's great to be back here!"

Everyone else looked baffled.

"Oh? Just me?" Uzuki sounded rattled.

"Zukki, what do you mean? Back here?" the short-haired girl on the other side of her asked.

"This is where we played our first-ever show!"

"……"

The other Sweet Bullet members and the audience settled into an awkward silence. Like a chill had swept through the room.

Even Uzuki realized something must be wrong.

"Wait, is this *not* there?" she asked, her smile faltering.

"We've never been here before," the short-haired girl whispered.

But with the mic held to her lips, so everyone could hear. Obviously intentional.

"You're kidding! Oh no! The aliens must have altered my memory!"

"Don't drag those poor aliens into this!" Nodoka yelled, laughing.

The crowd was laughing with them. Warm smiles everywhere. To their fans, this was clearly business as usual.

"Uh, so let's do another song! We've only got two numbers today, so no holding back!"

An enthusiastic recovery. The music kicked in.

"Sh-she's something else...," Kaede said. Her words speaking volumes.

"Yeah, she is. And she couldn't fit in at a conventional high school. That's how she wound up at a remote-learning place."

"Huh?"

"I went to an orientation behind your back, and they did a reel of student interviews. She was one of them. I checked with Toyohama, and she confirmed it."

"...Oh."

It sounded like she was saying that just to say something. Like it hadn't sunk it at all.

Perhaps it was difficult to connect that to someone who could sing, dance, smile like that, and goof up the moment she opened her mouth.

"As far as Minegahara goes..."

"......"

The moment he mentioned the name, Kaede's shoulders went stiff. She didn't even want to hear that word. Kaede was sure she'd messed up the exam, felt guilty for not trying harder to get through it. None of that was true.

"If *you* want to go, then I'll have your back forever."

"......But the exam's over."

"There's secondary admissions."

"......"

"But if you aren't actually the one who wants to go to Minegahara, then I don't feel a need to bend over backward to get you there. Mai and Toyohama agree with me. Dad and Ms. Tomobe are on the same page. And I'm sure the other Kaede would be, too."

"!"

"I think you oughtta find a life where the little things make you happy. The scrumptious scrambled eggs for breakfast, but sometimes they cook too fast and get all hard, and we laugh about how bad I messed them up, and maybe Mai teaches you the trick to make 'em yourself, and you struggle to learn. Laughing about nothing, enjoying the good times, today, tomorrow, and the day after that. That's all I want. I don't want you being obsessed with making *her* wishes come true."

It was a long speech, but his words never once faltered. He didn't need to stop and think. All of this was just waiting inside him. He'd been thinking these words over and over for ages.

"Sakuta…"

"Even if you get into Minegahara, if you've gotta punish yourself to go there, I'd be against it."

"Mm. It's just…"

Kaede trailed off.

"If there's something on your mind, it's best to say it," Sakuta said.

Kaede thought for a moment before she did.

"I do…want to do what everyone does."

Her voice was awfully quiet.

"Doing something else…is mortifying."

"Like that girl onstage?"

She'd certainly acted the ditz and got a big laugh. If Kaede had been in that position, she'd probably have died. Or at least run away.

"She's all kinds of amazing."

Uzuki's hair was flying out behind her. Beads of sweat spraying. Her smile lighting up the venue.

"But she's not like 'everyone.'"

"……"

Kaede started to answer, but the words caught in her throat. She dropped her gaze, lost in thought.

She stayed quiet as the bridge played, but when Uzuki started singing again, she said, "I dunno."

"Then let's talk to her, figure that out, and then look again at what *you* want to do."

He felt Kaede needed to know there was more to "everyone" than she thought. There were plenty of different crowds out there, and finding one she could get on with would be how she gained the courage and confidence she needed.

"Talk...?"

"I asked Toyohama. They've got time after this. Figured you could ask her about school and stuff."

"...And that's why we're here?" she asked, finally putting the pieces together.

Her eyes turned back to the stage.

She didn't outwardly accept or reject his plan. But the way she watched Uzuki's every move was all he needed.

"Sakuta," Kaede said, not glancing his way.

"Mm?"

"I really don't *have* to go to Minegahara?"

It would have been easy to just say yes. But this wasn't *his* choice. It was Kaede's. It was a choice she had to make to be herself, to become herself.

So he pretended like he was answering her question but actually said something else entirely.

"The other Kaede was always super dedicated."

"……"

"She woke up in a bed at the hospital, didn't know where she was or who any of us were. She must have been so lost."

"……Mm."

"And she did everything she could to be my little sister."

So that this time he wouldn't have regrets. Like he had from failing to help the original Kaede.

"And being my sister made me her brother."

"This other me was really something."

Her voice shook. She was biting her lip.

"When I realized she was gone, I was totally heartbroken. You won't believe how much I cried. I didn't even know I had that many tears in me."

Sakuta had bawled his eyes out. Feeling like he was squeezing out every last drop of moisture his body had in it.

"I still feel like crying when I remember her."

"So she was…"

He could see her head dropping out of the corner of his eye, so before she could finish that thought, he got to the important part.

"But, Kaede, as much as I cried, the other half of me was overjoyed. Happier than I'd ever been."

"Huh?"

"Because you'd come back."

He glanced her way and found Kaede looking at him, surprised. Tears welling up in her eyes.

"…You mean that?" she asked.

"Of course. Geez, you think I'm a monster?"

"How was I supposed to know? You gotta say these things out loud."

Kaede's tears were flowing now.

But her sobs were drowned out by Sweet Bullet's music.

"I thought you liked the other me better. That's why…"

Her tears pattered on the ground at their feet.

"I thought…I had to replace her…"

Sakuta put his hand on her head.

"I promise I don't like one of you over the other."

"…Really?"

"You're both just *whatever*."

"Oh, come on."

She looked up at him, her face a fright.

"You're both my *sisters*. You don't go around *liking* your sisters—that's creepy."

That seemed to make sense to her. The tears were still coming, but he got a smile out of her. And a real one. Not like the awkward half smiles she'd been prone to since she got her memories back.

The mini concert ended, and the stage area cleared out. In no time at all, the crowd was gone, too.

Only Sakuta and Kaede were left hanging out as the staff cleared the stage.

They were waiting to meet up with Nodoka.

Since they were *both* phoneless weirdos, vacating the area would make it impossible for anyone to find them.

Kaede had managed to stop crying, but her nose was still rather stuffy. She was about ready to run out of pocket tissues. He considered making a store run, but someone called his name.

A blond was waving at them from backstage, about thirty yards off. Nodoka. Probably inappropriate idol behavior, but none of the staff seemed to care.

Nodoka beckoned them over, and Uzuki Hirokawa was with her. Both were in street clothes now.

"Kaede, Toyohama's ready for us."

"Mm. Oh, wait, Sakuta."

"Mm?"

He'd taken a step forward, but he turned back to her.

"Can we go to the zoo sometime soon?" she asked, as soon as their eyes met.

"Well, we've gotta justify the membership fee," he said. The math insisted they had to go at *least* four times.

"I wanna see the pandas," she said, puffing up her cheeks in protest.

"You like pandas, too?"

He thought that was the other Kaede.

"I...respect them," she said, catching up to him. He had no idea what *that* meant, and his confusion must have showed, because she offered a supplemental explanation. "Everyone comes to see them, but they just don't care. Pandas are cool like that."

"Makes sense," he said. Maybe that's why the other Kaede liked them so much, too.

Nodoka was starting to look impatient, so they hustled over to her.

Chapter
4

Dare to Dream

1

He and Kaede had gone to see Sweet Bullet perform on a weekend, and that was followed by the final week of February. Monday would be the first day of March. And the day of the Minegahara graduation ceremony. To Sakuta's mind, that just meant Mai was graduating.

But even with that fated day a week out, Sakuta's daily routine hadn't changed at all.

Monday was business as usual, just like Mondays are the world over. The days after were no different.

Up in the morning, ready for school, leave early enough to get there on time. Pay attention in every class. Go to work when he had shifts, straight home otherwise.

Mai told him to study daily, so he did.

The only real change was that Kaede was once again going to the nurse's office at school. And after she got home, she was pouring over the remote-learning-center brochures. On top of that, she started a self-training program with the Internet and e-mail.

On Wednesday, Mai wrapped up her college exams flawlessly, and she brought Nodoka over to hang out.

"It's an older one, so I don't use it anymore. It's all yours, Kaede."

She'd arrived with a Wi-Fi-equipped laptop. And a random spare mouse.

The bullying she'd endured in junior high had involved a lot of e-mail and online abuse, directly leading to her Adolescence

Syndrome symptoms, so she was super wary about it at first. They put the laptop down on the *kotatsu*, and it took a good two or three minutes for her to work up the courage to sit down in front of it, and when she reached for the mouse and keyboard, her hands were shaking.

But Mai and Nodoka encouraged her the whole time, and after a few e-mails back and forth with them, she relaxed a bit, and her fingers grew steady. And each time she got a reply, her smile broadened.

Only Sakuta was left off-line and out of the loop. But he was just thrilled to see Kaede talking to both of them without him in the middle.

Eventually, Kaede said, "What are you smirking about, weirdo?" and Nodoka went, "Whatever he's thinking, it's dirty," and tried to kick him under the *kotatsu*. Naturally, he anticipated it and dodged in time.

Mai gave him a silent thigh pinch, but that was a reward, so he was honored to accept it.

All things considered, it was a big step toward getting Kaede back online. Modern society was pretty dependent on this stuff—enough that the word *IT* now felt *old*. It would be really hard for her to keep going without it. She'd need to get over her fears eventually, and if she was going to try the whole remote-learning thing, her schooling required it.

So he took it as a good sign when she went right from e-mailing Mai and Nodoka to accessing the homepages for various remote schools. She dug into the sites for the schools whose brochures had got her attention, trying to figure out which was best for her.

He knew Uzuki Hirokawa had played a big part in making her move forward. They'd talked for quite a while after the concert, and it had made a big impression on Kaede. And Sakuta had learned a few things listening to them.

On the day in question—Saturday, February 21—Sakuta and Kaede had gone to see Sweet Bullet perform at the Tsujido shopping mall, and after the event, Nodoka introduced them to Uzuki.

The second they met up, she said, "Let's get moving!" and led them over to the roundabout in front of the mall, to the lane for normal cars.

"Oh, there we go. That one!"

Uzuki raced forward to a navy-blue minivan, leaving them blinking in her wake. She opened the passenger-seat door and jumped in.

"All aboard!" she said, waving through the window.

While Sakuta and Kaede were exchanging glances, Nodoka slid the back door open. Then she took a seat in the third row of seats. Clearly waiting for them.

With no other options, they got in and sat down together in the second row.

"Seatbelts, please," the driver said. She was an outgoing-looking woman, maybe thirty. Hair to her shoulders, dyed a brighter shade. She was wearing jeans and a hoodie, super casual.

She kept her eyes on the mirror until she was sure everyone was buckled in, then said, "Here we go!" and drove off. Who was this lady?

"Um…," Sakuta said, attempting to inquire. Before he could, the idol in the passenger seat spun around and interrupted him.

"So, yeah, I'm Uzuki Hirokawa!" she said. She leaned all the way through the gap between the seats, holding her hand out toward them. It was obviously for a handshake.

It seemed rude to ignore this, so he said, "Sakuta Azusagawa," and took her hand. Uzuki immediately reached out her other hand and put it on top of his.

"Cool beans!" she said, moving the whole hand pile up and down twice.

"…Rad," Sakuta managed, and she flashed a smile, letting go.

"Uzuki Hirokawa!" she said, holding her hand toward Kaede.

"Er, r-right. Kaede Azusagawa." Kaede tentatively lifted her hand from her lap, and Uzuki leaned even further in to catch it. She wrapped both hands around it and shook the stack twice.

"Cool beans!"

"Uh, nice to meet you?"

Kaede was totally bowled over. Overwhelmed.

He'd thought this while watching her onstage as well, but Uzuki's idea of appropriate distancing was definitely a bit unusual. She just started right up close.

And she didn't let go of Kaede after the shake. She was looking from one to the other.

"Hmm," she said. Then rattled off, "If you're both Azusagawa, then Sakuta's the older brother, and Kaede's the younger sister, right? I'm the same age as Nodoka—which means we're equals! First-name basis it is! That work for you?"

She was hard to keep up with.

From the seat behind them, he heard Nodoka let out a sigh, half exasperated, half just tired. Real "she's at it again" energy. Maybe just not sure where Uzuki got this much pep right after a show.

"Er, um…," Kaede said, gaping back at her. She looked at Sakuta for help.

"I'm gonna stick with Hirokawa," he said.

"I'll go with Uzuki," Kaede said, her voice tiny.

"Aww," Uzuki said. "You can call me Zukki if you want!"

"I do so in my heart," Sakuta admitted.

"Great!" she said, cackling. "Same for Doka?"

That was Nodoka's nickname.

"Obviously."

"Don't!" Nodoka's voice came from behind.

He turned around to find her sitting in the center of the rear seat, scowling at him.

"Toyohama," he said.

"What?"

"I see France."

"?!"

She let out a voiceless shriek.

She had on a short skirt and boots and had taken off her jacket when she stepped into the car, leaving bare thighs all the way up. The skirt was black, so that patch of light blue stood out.

"Oh, you totally can!" Uzuki chimed in.

"Yours are equally on display, Uzuki," the driver said. "You're in a miniskirt! Keep those legs together."

"But if I don't brace myself, I can't turn around."

"It's hardly safe! Face forward right now!"

They'd just stopped at a red light, so the driver grabbed Uzuki's collar and sat her down.

In the rearview mirror, he could see Nodoka putting her down jacket on her knees. Her glare stabbing into the back of Sakuta's head. It wasn't *his* fault he'd gotten an eyeful, but clearly she blamed him anyway. Kaede was radiating silent protest, and the driver seemed to be enjoying this awkward silence.

As they pulled out, Sakuta said, "By the way, Hirokawa…" like nothing had happened. It seemed silly to dwell on this subject for long.

"Whaaat?" she said, somehow making even that word over-the-top.

"This is important."

"Oh? Asking me out already?"

"Who's this lady?" he asked, jerking a thumb at the driver and completely ignoring her assumption.

The driver kept her eyes on the road, driving safely.

Uzuki slapped her on the shoulders. "Lady? She's my mom!"

"Don't—I'm driving. Stop that!"

When they cleared the curve, she flicked Uzuki's forehead, then glanced into the rearview mirror.

"But I *am* Uzuki's mom."

Their eyes met, so he bobbed his head. She did *not* look like she had a daughter in high school.

"How old *are* you?" he asked, putting his query in words.

"How old do I look?"

"Never mind, then."

It was *not* worth dealing with that response.

"I had Uzuki when I was eighteen," she said, laughing. So she was in her midthirties. Her hair, clothes, and friendly disposition all conspired to make her look younger. Despite her daughter's age, it kinda made sense.

"Didn't you wanna ask about school?" Uzuki's mom prompted, sensing they weren't getting anywhere.

"Oh, right! Kaede, ask away!" Uzuki said, attempting to turn around again. Her mother caught her midturn and forced her back in her seat.

"You stay put! You're not a child!"

"I *am*, though!"

They certainly seemed close. Sakuta and Kaede didn't even *live* with their parents, so it was dazzling to watch.

"......"

Kaede was just watching them without a word. Probably thinking the same thing he was.

The whole bullying thing had caused her Adolescence Syndrome, and then her dissociative disorder had taken her memories. One problem after another had whittled away at their mother's confidence. Living together had proved inadvisable, and that had not gotten better.

And Kaede blamed herself.

"Kaede, if you've got questions, better ask them," he said, shaking those feelings off.

"Oh, uh. Mm, I just…"

"If you're going, 'But Hirokawa is nothing like me,' well, nobody's like anyone else, so pay that no never mind."

"Wow, your brother's a smart cookie!"

"Er, um, Uzuki, why—?" Kaede was interrupted by the blare of a passing car horn.

But nobody here—not Sakuta, Nodoka, Uzuki, or her mom—tried to rush her. They just waited for her to try again.

"Uzuki, what made you choose this school?"

Kaede finally got it out as the car hit the coast road—Route 134, headed for Kamakura.

Uzuki didn't answer right away. She made a bunch of thinking noises, though.

As they reached the next light, she said, "'Cause Mom found it for me?" like she was asking the question. Maybe asking herself.

"Don't answer questions with questions!" her mom snapped.

"Uh, but that's kinda it? I'd stopped going to school entirely, so you gave me that brochure and said, 'Quit that dumb place and go here.' Oh, did you know I started at a regular school?"

"I know what you said in the video."

Uzuki had been the capper on the PR film shown at the orientation he and Miwako had attended. She'd talked about failing to make friends at her original school and gradually attending less and less. It didn't sound like she'd had problems like Kaede; no mean e-mails or messages. Just passive indifference.

"I didn't start skipping in high school, either. It was in junior high— around when I started the whole idol thing. All these lessons we've gotta do—I never had time to hang with classmates."

"And if you turn too many invites down, girls stop inviting you at all," Nodoka chimed in. It sounded like she knew from personal experience.

"I know, right?!" Uzuki said.

Sakuta glanced over his shoulder as she did. His eyes briefly met Nodoka's, but she soon looked away.

He'd heard before that she didn't really fit in at her fancy girls' school and wasn't exactly enjoying her time there. But she kept going because her mother wanted her to. To whatever extent she could, Nodoka wanted to please her mother. She might've been bucking against her, to the point where she'd left home and was living with Mai instead, but deep down, there was still love there.

"I hoped I could do better in high school, but…summer vacation ended, second term began, and I just gave up. Everyone had spent that vacation doing stuff together, and I didn't have a clue what they were talking about."

Her tone stayed upbeat, and her phrasing cheery. But behind her words was an undeniable sense of regret, which she was trying to plaster over with empty half smiles.

"At first, I only meant to take one day off. But then I took the next day off, and the day after…and just never went back."

She broke off, lost in memory, eyes on the window. Enoshima was on their right. The sun dipping lower in the west, turning the sky orange. It was a view that could sell a million postcards.

Gazing at that, Sakuta found himself asking, "And how did that make your mom feel?"

His question must have seemed like it came out of the blue, but Uzuki's mom didn't bat an eye.

"Honestly, I was kinda at a loss."

She made it sound jokey. Her eyes momentarily caught Sakuta's in the mirror.

"At the time, I'd been a mom a good fifteen or sixteen years but sure hadn't dealt with a dropout before. Didn't know what to say to her, and anyone I could have asked would have just spouted conventional wisdom back at me. I didn't know what to do with her. Total wit's-end scenario. And I didn't really do much of anything. Maybe that makes me a bad mother."

"I don't think it does," Sakuta said, before anyone else could.

If he hadn't seen what happened to his own mother, he might still have thought they were omnipotent. Creatures capable of solving all their kids' problems without breaking a sweat.

But Uzuki's mother had it right. You could be a parent as long as your kids were old and still come across new issues. Overcoming these one at a time, growing with their kids—that was how moms became moms and dads became dads.

And some of those problems weren't overcome. Parents had their limits, too. Sakuta's parents had taught him that. Just as deeply unfair things could happen to kids, deeply unreasonable demands were placed upon their parents.

"It was *way* easier on me that she never tried to make me go back. I don't think she said a word about it."

"Not like I was huge on the place myself. I may not look it now, but I had my wild years."

"Don't worry, you totally look it."

Sakuta was just being honest.

"You're a fun one, Sakuta," she said, laughing. And then she got serious again. "But, well…part of me thought, 'There's no point going to school if you don't wanna be there.' But another part of me felt like I should at least get her to graduate. Me and my man ain't gonna be hung up on no diplomas, but you can't make a living as an idol your whole life, can you?"

"I will!" Uzuki said, leaning in.

"Basically, parents are *gonna* worry," her mom said, pushing Uzuki's face away.

Every interaction these two had proved how tight they were.

"Nodoka, your mom worries, too!"

Nodoka made a noise somewhere between an "Ugh" and a sigh.

"Are you at least visiting?"

"I stopped by over New Year's. She wouldn't quit texting me."

"You know she was at the concert today?"

"I saw her from the stage."

Nodoka's tone made it clear she couldn't just be *happy* about that. But she *had* noticed.

There'd been something like three hundred people there. It wasn't easy to find *one* person in a crowd that size. So if Nodoka had found her mother, she must have known she'd be there, and Nodoka had looked for her. And she was acting grumpy because she knew what a contradiction that was. And was ashamed of it.

"But we're not here about me! Sakuta, eyes front."

He didn't want to derail this any further, either, so he turned around.

"Uh, so back to the point. I figured if we could find a school Uzuki would *want* to go to, she should. So I looked into remote learning, part-time education, overseas schools… I gave you a bunch of brochures."

She turned on her right blinker. When the oncoming traffic slowed, she spun the wheel and pulled into a parking lot by the shore. It looked familiar.

"You handle the rest. I'll be waiting in the café there."

When the car stopped, she engaged the parking brake and got out. He didn't even have time to go, "Here...?"

And so he reluctantly clambered out. The girls followed.

"Of all the places," he muttered.

The parking lot faced the ocean. The same ocean he saw every day. For good reason. It was the lot right across from Minegahara High.

It was the off-season, so there were only a handful of scattered cars, a dozen yards or so apart.

"Wow, Zukki. Living up to your rep for cluelessness."

"Mm? What, is something wrong?" Uzuki asked, blinking at her.

Ignorance could cause mishaps like this.

"I told you!"

"What?"

Nodoka flung an arm over her shoulders and whispered in her ear, which made Uzuki go, "Augh!"

This was loud enough that a nearby couple spun around in surprise. Kaede flinched and hid behind Sakuta.

"Sorry, Kaede!"

Uzuki slapped her hands together, bowing as if in prayer.

"Seriously, totally my bad! Augh, Mom's already in the shop."

"I-it's fine! It just startled me. But less than you'd think. And..."

Kaede peeled away from Sakuta and faced the ocean. The same view you saw from the windows of the school. The beach at Shichirigahama.

"I wanted to see the beach here."

"Really? Then should we hit the sand?"

"I-I'd like that."

"Come on, come on!"

Back in good spirits, Uzuki led the way down the stairs. Nodoka followed, grumbling in Kaede's place.

"Not your fault, Nodoka!"

"It never was!"

Sakuta and Kaede followed after them.

"You're sure about this, Kaede?" he asked, still concerned.

"I did want to see the beach. I swear, I wanted to come here."

She was being pretty forceful.

"Well, good."

He looked back ahead and saw Nodoka and Uzuki struggling with the heels of their boots in the sand.

"Don't fall," he said.

"I'm! Doing! Fine!"

"We can handle it!"

Neither answer was remotely convincing. He watched, half-lidded...

"Ack, whoops!" and Uzuki lost her balance.

She caught Nodoka's arm for support, but Nodoka didn't have herself braced enough for that, and they both landed on their butts.

"Don't drag me into your catastrophes!"

"Idols are ride and die!" Uzuki said, apparently having the time of her life.

"This isn't *fun*!" Nodoka said, brushing sand away.

"Well, the school I'm at now *is*," Uzuki said, not getting up. She turned, looking at Kaede over her shoulder. A delighted smile on her face.

There was basically no transition there, but apparently, she'd jumped back to the earlier topic.

"At first, honestly, I was *not* into the idea. At all. Mom had to drag me to the orientation. I mean, does *anyone* have a positive image of remote learning?"

Uzuki did a patented flashback smile. Like any second now she'd say something about how young she'd been.

"I was so young then!"

She actually *did*.

"But everyone's like that," Nodoka agreed.

"Everyone's like what?" Sakuta asked.

She glared at him. Clearly a "you know, so don't ask" look.

"Bracing themselves when they hear *remote learning* or *part-time education*," she said, reluctantly spelling it out.

Kaede was certainly nodding. Those opinions were a major concern. That's what everyone else thought. Uzuki's classmates had accused her of never reading the room, but even *she'd* been aware of it. That was simply proof of how widely held that sentiment was.

Biased perceptions and feelings can take root in the soil of social spaces. Normal, ordinary, majority-side people just assume that their position is always *right*. They just prefer it that way. That makes things easier for them, and by putting down anyone different, they in turn feel safe. This was how people convince themselves their position is secure.

They don't even realize they're looking down on anyone. None of them have any clue their biases hurt others. Because *everyone* does it all the time.

"I didn't really realize it until it became the plan, you know? Then the realer it got, the more uncomfortable I was. Like I didn't want anyone knowing about it. And that made it hard to, like, talk to anyone about it."

"I think not having to go to school every day sounds just about perfect," Sakuta said.

"The last thing anyone who can actually *do* that gets to say," Uzuki said, dramatically pointing at him, like a referee calling a foul.

She seemed so outgoing it was easy to forget, but that response made it clear just how rough her relationship with schooling had been. He'd caught a brief glimpse of something he couldn't laugh off.

"Fair enough," he said, taking it back.

"I mean, it's sweet that you think that," Uzuki said, grinning. All trace of reproach was gone. Whatever problems she'd had were over and done with now.

"Going to the orientation really turned me around," Sakuta said. "They made it clear that my preconceptions were way off base."

"I know! That did it for me. Not even kidding, that totally changed my whole idea of what school could be."

"Oh yeah. Definitely."

Including his ideas about conventional schools.

"I thought *school* meant a set time and place, same people, same classes. Everything set in stone, and you *had* to join in."

"...Is that not true?" Kaede asked, like this was all new to her.

"It's not *wrong*! That's how conventional schools do it, and I never even questioned that. 'Everyone else does just fine with that, so it must be my fault that I can't.' And that was suffocating."

Kaede's eyes never left Uzuki. As if sympathizing with that feeling, she clamped her hands together. To Sakuta, it looked like she was enduring that same "suffocating" sensation.

"But the orientation my mom dragged me to—they said it didn't have to be that way. That conventional education techniques were not the only right answer. That we didn't have to shape ourselves to our schools but could find a school that fit us, that let us make our own choices. So I was like, '*That's* too good to be true.'"

"Same." Sakuta nodded.

"I thought that, but I also felt like it was up to me what I made of it. If mean, if I can study when I want, where I want, then I don't have to skip school for idol stuff, and that sounded ideal!"

"Every break we take leaves us further on the fringe of class," Nodoka growled. Clearly a thing she'd long since given up on.

"So you decided to enroll after the orientation?" Sakuta prompted.

She had to think about that one. Like she was feeling out her own emotions, hunting for what she wanted Kaede to hear.

"I think I made up my mind in the car going home. Part of me was like, 'It might be cool,' and another part was still going, 'But remote learning?' But then my mom was like, 'When I got knocked up, everyone around me said I shouldn't have you.' That wasn't some TV show, but everyone was actually like, 'Kids can't raise kids!'"

Normally, pregnancy was cause for celebration, but slap the word *teenage* in front of it, and it sure hit different. The world did not approve. And like with Uzuki's mom, lots of times, no one gave their blessings. Probably *most* times.

Teenage or not, some people would make good moms, and some people wouldn't. Age was not the only dividing line. Remote learning, teenage pregnancy, or anything else—popular opinion was often based on preconceptions and prejudice and was so distorted by prevailing mores that nobody could see the truth.

"But she did a pretty bang-up job raising you," Sakuta concluded.

"Mm!" Uzuki nodded enthusiastically. "Everyone was against it, but Mom had me anyway and brought me up just fine. And that got me thinking about the definition of *everyone*. I got super serious and asked her, 'Who is *everyone*?'"

"And what did your mom say?" Nodoka asked.

Uzuki was grinning before she even answered. "'Uzuki, your happiness isn't dictated by everyone. It's what *you* say it is.'"

"Your mom's a badass."

"I know! She's too cool for school."

In the car, she'd said she didn't know what to say when her daughter dropped out of school. But what she'd actually said was so *deep*. The words of a mother who'd had Uzuki at only eighteen and been a mom ever since—they weren't merely convincing. Sakuta could feel them sinking deep inside him.

"Wish I had a mom like yours," Nodoka muttered. "You're so close."

"Yeah? But your mom's lovely! All elegant. My mom was still dying her hair blond when I was in grade school, rolling into Parents' Day in a tracksuit and sandals. So cringe."

"Ugh, yeah, wouldn't want."

Nodoka about-faced quick.

"See? And she can't cook at all."

"Should you be telling us that?" Sakuta asked.

Uzuki spun toward him. "Don't tell her I did! I'll get no dinner."

She sounded genuinely alarmed. Like that had not been an empty threat and she'd been punished that way before.

"But, uh, in a roundabout way, it was your mom who convinced you to try this school," Nodoka said, getting the conversation back on track.

"But also you, Nodoka," Uzuki said, turning to look her right in the eye.

"Huh?" Nodoka just blinked at her, totally lost.

"You and everyone in Sweet Bullet. Even when I'd quit school, you were all there for me. You and the fans."

Uzuki shifted to face the ocean, thoughts running to people not present.

"I couldn't get on with the kids at school. But I had the other group members, my fans, and my mom with me. And having all those things made it possible for me to try this new school. Mm. I know that's true."

She was looking out at the horizon. From average standing height, that was only three miles out. Closer than you'd think. Uzuki was sitting on the sand, so it was even less. Close enough to walk to. Sakuta thought that was a good length. It was tough to go chasing a goal you couldn't see. Much better to run toward something you could. Just make it to the next telephone pole. Keep doing that, and eventually, you'd find yourself beyond that horizon, somewhere you'd never seen before.

Uzuki had wrapped things up by convincing herself of her own answer, but when nobody else said anything, she leaned in, whispering in Nodoka's ear.

"Did that answer Kaede's question?"

They were sitting close enough that everyone heard.

"With extra credit," Sakuta said.

Kaede nodded.

"Really? I don't get these things, so tell me if I'm off the mark! Anything else you wanna know? Ask away!"

"......Then just one more?"

"As many as you like!"

"Which...version of yourself do you like better? When you were at a normal school, or this one?"

Kaede sounded a bit tense. She clearly wanted the latter answer and was expecting Uzuki to say just that. But Sakuta saw a different answer coming—and knew that was a good thing.

"I like 'em both the same!" Uzuki said, not even wavering. Her eyes on Kaede's. "What the old me did made me who I am now."

That made Kaede gape. She might have looked stunned, but he

knew that was the face she made when the needle dropped. As proof, she closed her jaw, then smiled like it all made sense.

"Oh. Right."

"Right!"

"Uh…thank you," Kaede said, bobbing her head.

"You're welcome! I sure talked a lot. I think I figured some things out myself here! So thank you."

Uzuki held out her hand. Kaede hesitated for a moment but wound up shaking Uzuki's hands for the second time that day.

After that, they'd hit up the café where Uzuki's mom was waiting, warmed up with hot beverages, and talked more about the specifics of Uzuki's school.

Uzuki pulled out her phone and played back some of the videos and showed off the chat logs from one of the morning homeroom sessions—as well as some club stuff also done in chat rooms and some promo videos that students had made to recruit club members.

All of this was on the tiny screen of her phone. But you could feel the warmth of the students involved.

A school in the palm of your hand. In there were teachers, students, lessons, classmates, and friendships.

They just weren't in the same physical location. And if you thought about it, as online as everything was these days, that was hardly strange.

Yet he could feel himself instinctively balking at the idea that *this* was high school. Without him ever realizing it, the bias against that idea had been drilled into him.

Naturally, not all remote-learning schools operated like what Uzuki had shown them. But the school she went to matched his ideas of what a school was. The feel of the students convinced him of that.

"The declining birth rate means the number of schools is just gonna keep on shrinking," Uzuki's mom said. "More and more students will be stuck without a school close enough to them. By the time all of you have kids in high school, taking classes on phones and computer screens might be mainstream."

"I'm attending the school of the future," Uzuki added. She winked playfully, but she also sounded proud.

And that enthusiasm, combined with everything they'd talked about that day—it had all meant a lot to Kaede. It had all spoken to her.

And that was why, on Friday, February 27, only two days till the month changed over—

"Sakuta."

"Mm?"

"I'd like to go to the orientation here."

He'd just stepped out of the bath and found Kaede waiting with a brochure in hand. The same school Sakuta and Miwako had gone to visit—in other words, the one Uzuki attended.

"I'll ask Ms. Tomobe when the next meeting is."

"I checked their homepage. There's one every Sunday in March."

She pulled the laptop across the *kotatsu*, showing him the screen. They had orientations on the first, eighth, fifteenth, and twenty-second.

"The Internet sure is a time saver."

"Mm."

"But the first is graduation… Can it wait till the eighth?"

"Mai's graduating, so I'm not about to insist we gotta go then."

She looked annoyed he'd even suggest that.

"But I've got you reserved for the eighth!" she said, clearly pleased with herself.

"Okay, okay," Sakuta said, grabbing a sports drink from the fridge.

2

The next day was Saturday the twenty-eighth—the last day of February. And Kaede was rushing him all the way to Fujisawa Station.

"Sakuta, hurry! Komi might be there already!"

Kaede was using her nickname for Kotomi Kano, a friend from when they'd still lived in Yokohama. Both families had lived in the same apartment complex, so they'd played together since before either could remember. *Kotomi* had become *Komi* because Kaede had been so little that she couldn't wrap her tongue around that many sounds. For the same reason, *Kaede* had been shorted to *Kae*.

Kotomi had visited once over winter vacation and had left her e-mail address on an "if you feel up to it" basis. And last night, Kaede had initiated contact. They'd gone back and forth a few times and decided to meet up today.

That might sound like a hasty arrangement, but his plans with Mai were frequently no more complex than:

"You free today, Sakuta?"

"Yep."

"Then it's a date!"

So he just figured that was how these things went sometimes.

At Fujisawa Station, Sakuta and Kaede headed for the JR gates. A train must have just come in, because a flood of people was pouring out.

"Oh, Komi! There she is."

Kaede found her first and started waving.

Kotomi saw them and hustled over. She stood right in front of Kaede, took both hands, and said, "Kae! Finally!"

She sounded delighted.

"Mm. Thanks for coming!"

"I had to. Anytime! I can't believe you actually e-mailed me."

One look at her eyes made it clear she meant every word. They were glistening with tears, like the joy of that moment was still with her.

Kotomi knew all about the bullying at Kaede's previous junior high. They'd both gone there.

They'd been in different classes, and Kotomi had bitterly regretted being unable to help.

And on top of that, Kaede's dissociative disorder had meant the two of them moved out without even saying good-bye.

It must have been a huge loss to her.

But that was exactly why she was so glad she could see Kaede again and even e-mail her.

And the emotions had Kaede misting up a bit, too.

She may have struggled with her classmates, but she still had real friends left. Like Kotomi, people who liked her as she was.

He didn't want to go around looking for the silver lining in that whole mess, but it had taught Kaede who actually mattered to her. And that was why she'd followed up her practice session with Mai and Nodoka by e-mailing Kotomi. She wanted to see her again. And Kotomi felt the same way.

"Sakuta, thanks for coming," Kotomi said, bowing her head to him. She wiped tears away under her glasses.

"It's cool. I need to pick up some rice and soy sauce at the store on the way back anyway."

"I'm happy to help carry!"

He'd been half joking, but Kotomi tended to take these things seriously.

By the time they got back to the apartment, each lugging a bag of groceries, the clock read 11:10. They led Kotomi into the living room and put some tea in front of her.

Sakuta changed clothes in his bedroom and then went to the kitchen to get lunch ready. Potatoes, carrots, onions—these could wind up as curry *or* stew. Kotomi saw him at it and offered to help.

"You're company! Sit down."

"Let me help."

Before he could say anything else, Kotomi started washing her hands. If she was that motivated, it seemed silly to argue.

He had her start peeling.

Kaede usually never helped, but she couldn't well just sit there watching. They wound up making curry together like it was a home ec class.

The finished product sure had a variety of veggie sizes and textures.

They hadn't had time to let it simmer, so the roux was kinda watery. But it was weirdly good despite that.

"Kae, this is so good."

"Mm, I know!"

The girls were super proud of their work.

"We might have made a bit too much, though…"

Kotomi glanced at the stockpot on the stove.

"It's enough for three days even we eat it for all three meals."

"It's good, but not *that* good," Kaede said, quickly revising her opinion downward.

"I'll just make Mai and Toyohama come over to help."

If he told them Kaede made it, they'd be only too happy to join in. Mai would probably scold him for using his sister as an excuse, but that was just killing two—maybe three!—birds with one stone. They'd totally have to throw a curry party after graduation tomorrow.

Once lunch was over, Sakuta handled cleanup. While he was doing dishes, the girls sat at the *kotatsu*, looking at her laptop.

From the fragments of conversation he caught, they were talking about high school. Kaede was showing Kotomi the homepage for the remote-learning school she was interested in.

Kaede had clearly been very worried about how Kotomi would react. "Wow, this school really offers a lot of subjects!" Kotomi said, sounding genuinely impressed. And that loosened Kaede up enough to tell her all about what she'd gleaned from meeting Uzuki Hirokawa.

"That's really something."

"Yeah, they have so many options—"

"No, I mean you, Kae."

"Huh?"

"I didn't pick my school like this. I didn't research it or anything. My teacher just said, 'With your grades, you should consider this one' and I just went with it. You're way more independent."

Kaede had not expected this compliment and turned bright red, but even from the kitchen, he could tell she was tickled pink.

Sakuta thought Kotomi coming over at this juncture was the right move. It put wind in Kaede's sails just as she'd finally started moving forward.

When he was done washing up, Sakuta retreated to his room to change again. He had a shift starting at three.

He poked his head into the living room on his way out and found Kaede and Kotomi still at the *kotatsu* together. Still peering at the laptop screen. But they were now watching videos of goats screaming or cats that wanted to sit on top of the TV. Kotomi catching Kaede up on the latest viral vids.

"Oh, this one's also really big right now."

Kotomi clicked the search bar and loaded up another video site.

As Sakuta peered over their shoulders, he caught the poster's name: Touko Kirishima.

"Touko Kirishima?" Kaede said, reading it aloud.

"Mm. Really pretty visuals, and the song's nice, too."

Kotomi clicked the play button, and the trippy visuals were accompanied by heartrending music.

It was a different song and video from the one Mai had shown him. If Kotomi knew it, the girl's work must have been *really* popular.

"I'm off to work," he said.

"Oh, right. Have a good one," Kotomi said, looking back.

"Kano, make sure you get home before dark."

"I plan to."

"Sakuta, you'd better get going."

Kotomi bowed her head, and Kaede gave him a wave. He moved to the door and was putting his shoes on when the phone rang. Their home phone.

He turned back and found Kaede out of the *kotatsu*, in front of the phone. Peering at the screen from one step too far back.

They knew that number.

"Ms. Miwako, right?" Kaede said, checking with him.

"Yeah," he said, reaching for the receiver. Before he could…

"Can I answer?" Kaede asked.

"As long as it isn't Mai, you can pick up for whoever you want."

He pulled his hand away, giving her room. Kaede stepped closer, took a deep breath, and picked up the receiver.

"H-hello? Azusagawa speaking." Her voice broke on the first syllable. After a moment, she continued, "Yes, it's Kaede. He's here, but…it was your number, so I figured… Yes."

She seemed to be conversing just fine.

"Okay. Right…"

He couldn't hear Miwako's end, so he had no idea what this was about.

"Huh? I *passed*?"

This only made Kaede's surprise all the more shocking for him. Kotomi was watching over her from the *kotatsu* and appeared equally startled. Her eyes met Sakuta's, exchanging quizzical looks.

But Kaede had just said *passed*.

Passed what?

Or who…?

He was lost.

Kaede was just saying "Okay…okay…" over and over. It didn't sound like her emotions had caught up yet. Her mind was clearly elsewhere.

"Kae…?" Kotomi called.

"Kaede?" Sakuta asked.

"Passing you to Sakuta," Kaede squeaked, and she handed him the phone.

It would undoubtedly be faster to talk to Miwako directly.

"This is Sakuta. Ms. Tomobe?"

"Oh, Sakuta…you need me to catch you up?"

She heard the query in his voice.

"Yes, please."

"Short version…"

"Yes?"

"Kaede got into Minegahara."

"……"

"She passed."

"Hng?"

He made a very odd noise.

He couldn't believe his ears.

Kaede passed.

At Minegahara.

"How?" he asked, voicing the first question that came to mind.

"Pretty simple, really. They just came in under quota."

"I thought it was supposed to be competitive?"

Even if the actual percentage cutoff was lower than expected, it hadn't seemed like the number of applicants would go below the number of slots available. The famous Mai Sakurajima went there, so the school itself was pretty well-known…

"Initial applicants were actually twice that number."

"Then what happened?"

"Everyone realized they only had a fifty-fifty shot of getting in, so lots of people changed their target school. More than ever have before. Apparently, rumors were running wild on social media, panic mongering about how it was impossible for anyone to get in."

"…Really."

Everyone got caught up in the notion that they'd be in trouble if they didn't switch. The idea preyed on their already raw nerves.

"But however she did it, Kaede's in."

"Okay."

"But you need her ticket to receive the formal notification. Do you still have it?"

"I'd have to check with Kaede."

He hadn't seen it since the day of the test. When he'd picked up her things for her.

"There's lots of paperwork, so once you figure out what you want to do, get in touch."

"Okay. I'll have a long talk with her."

"Please do. Bye."

"Bye."

"Oh, wait…"

"What?"

"Congratulations."

"I'm not the one who passed."

"I already told Kaede."

And with that, Miwako hung up.

Her words hung in his head. The warmth with which she'd said "Congratulations." He wasn't used to having family members with anything to celebrate, and it felt weird. But it was extra welcome precisely because it wasn't *his* deed.

Words could do that. It felt like a new discovery.

He put the phone down and turned slowly around.

Kaede was staring right at him. Her gaze sent a strong message. He knew what she wanted.

He didn't need to ask.

But she still opened her mouth to speak. "Sakuta, I…"

And what she said next was exactly what he expected.

3

Sakuta was already running behind, so he abandoned the idea of rushing to work and called the restaurant. He explained what had happened and got permission to delay his start by an hour. With that taken care of, he called his dad.

Kaede's choice was clear, but this was her future, so best to loop their dad in. He'd want to be asked.

His dad soon picked up, but before Sakuta could even say a word, he asked, "The quota thing?"

He must have been even more hung up on it than Sakuta was and paying close attention to the prefectural admissions news.

"Ms. Tomobe called. Said we should make up our minds quick and start the paperwork."

"I figured I'd call about that this evening."

"Can you swing by tomorrow?"

"Okay. In the evening, after I see your mother in the hospital."

"Then I'll let Ms. Tomobe know we'll get her our answer Monday."

"Okay. I'll let you handle that."

"I told her I'd keep her updated."

"Good, you do that."

His father's voice was low. The signal itself was fine; he was intentionally keeping quiet. That made it clear where he was—their mother's hospital.

Her nerves had deteriorated after everything with Kaede. He didn't want her hearing this.

"See you tomorrow," Sakuta said, figuring the details could wait.

He hung up and called Miwako back to let her know they'd hash out the details tomorrow with their dad and call again on Monday.

When he finally put the phone down, it was three thirty.

Since his shift now started at four, it was still a bit early to leave. He wound up having some tea and a few of the cookies Kotomi had brought with her.

"Thanks," he said, finishing the last of his tea. "Okay, this time I really am going to work."

He peeled himself out from under the *kotatsu*.

"Oh, then I'll walk with you," Kotomi said, getting up, too. "Mom said I shouldn't outstay my welcome."

"You wouldn't be!" Kaede said, clearly not ready to part.

But Kotomi lived in the suburbs of Yokohama—twenty minutes on the Tokaido Line from Fujisawa Station, but then she had to take a different train bound inland, so the whole commute took about an hour. Getting back was no small feat.

"Let's have her sleep over the next time she visits," Sakuta suggested.

Kaede nodded. "I'll e-mail you!" she said.

And saw them off at the door.

Sakuta and Kotomi headed for the station. It was almost four, and the sun dropped toward the horizon. A week ago, the chill of night would already have been in the air, but now the sunlight felt almost warm.

Tomorrow was March 1. It was high time the world gave up this winter thing.

When they reached the main drag, they got caught by a red light.

"Kae's really something," Kotomi said.

"Yeah?"

"So mature."

"Is she...?"

He didn't know what she meant by that.

"Choosing her own school. Again."

"Oh, the Minegahara thing?"

He finally caught her drift.

Kaede had looked right at him, absolutely certain.

——*"Sakuta, I'm not going to Minegahara. I'm gonna find a school I want to go to."*

"If that had been me, I think I'd have jumped at the chance to go to a normal school."

"Because doing what everyone does is better?"

"Yeah."

"Kaede just happened to meet the right people."

He'd just happened to know someone she could talk to about remote learning. And that person being Uzuki Hirokawa was pretty key. Uzuki's mom had likely played just as big a role.

"But point taken. She took what she learned and did good."

"Make sure you tell her that. She'll be delighted."

"Ew. It'll just go to her head."

"Then I'll pass it along for you."

He glanced her way, and she already had her phone out. He saw her fingers dance across the screen.

"I just e-mailed it to her," she said, before he could stop her. "Oh, and she answered."

"Yeah?"

Kotomi read it and laughed.

"'Then he must be an imposter.'"

She showed him the screen as proof.

"Kaede's getting real witty these days."

Perhaps that was her growing up and becoming more mature.

The light turned green, and they started walking again.

The rest of the walk, they talked about Sakuta's job. Kotomi was thinking about getting one herself in high school. She was a smart kid and would probably do fine no matter where she worked.

They reached the station, and he saw her to the gates.

She bowed her head low, tapped her train pass, and went through. Then she turned back.

"I'll come stay over spring break," she said as she smiled and waved.

Sakuta raised a hand in response, and she dashed off down to the platform.

When she was out of sight, he turned toward the restaurant he worked at.

"Is that gonna make Mai mad...?"

Was having a sister's friend sleep over verboten or not? It was kinda hard to tell where the line lay.

Since they'd let him delay his shift an hour, he took the job a mite more seriously than usual. Swiftly busing emptied tables and saying "I'll get them" proactively when he saw someone at the register— letting his manager *know*.

After a while, there were more empty tables than not. Teatime was over, but the dinner rush hadn't started yet.

Sakuta was wiping down an empty table when the manager called out, "Sakuta, take your break now."

"You're sure? I *was* an hour late."

"Kunimi's already here, so you're good. Uh, but make it thirty. By then, it'll be filling up."

"That works."

He wasn't about to refuse a break.

He headed to the back of the shop, where he helped himself to the staff beverages.

"Sakuta," someone called. He knew it was Yuuma Kunimi without looking.

"What?"

"Turn this way."

"Why?"

Reluctantly turning around, he found Yuuma holding a tray with a chocolate parfait on it.

"Is that for me? I'd rather have a burger."

"There's a cutie at table six," Yuuma said, pushing the tray into his hands.

"Mai?" he asked.

But Yuuma just said, "You'll see." Then a bell rang—a customer trying to order. "Coming!" he called, and he moved away.

Yuuma probably wouldn't have used *cutie* with Mai. *Pretty* or *a beauty* maybe—those descriptors fit her better.

No point just standing around holding a parfait, and he *was* curious, so he headed to the table in question.

Table six had a girl in a junior high uniform, on her own in a booth meant for four.

When she saw Sakuta coming, her face lit up.

"Oh, Sakuta!" she squealed, her voice echoing across the room.

It was Shouko Makinohara.

He put the parfait down in front of her.

"Your chocolate parfait," he said.

"Wow!" she said, eyes glittering.

He sat down across from her. "What's up?"

"Do you have time?" she asked, searching his face.

"I'm actually on break."

"Oh, am I interrupting?"

Her eyes were already back on the dessert, though.

"We can talk while you eat."

"Okay!"

She grabbed her spoon, made sure she had ice cream, whipped cream, and chocolate on it, and popped into her mouth. Bliss spread to every inch of her features. Overall, she seemed the picture of health. Her heart transplant surgery had finally made that possible.

"You're looking good."

"The surgery was a *year* ago."

She tapped her chest, looking proud.

"This is all Mai! That movie did wonders."

"It sure made waves."

This movie was one Mai had made in junior high. It was released just before her hiatus and proved to be a huge hit tearjerker.

Mai had really thrown herself into the role of a girl with heart problems who hoped for a donor heart but had only a few months left to live. It was the exact same condition Shouko had.

"The doctors said the registered donor lists skyrocketed after that movie came out."

"Well, good."

"Do you think Mai remembered me?"

"No. Like me, she didn't remember anything until we were on our way back from the New Year's shrine visit. When we ran into you on the beach at Shichirigahama."

"Then why'd she take the role? Before the redo, she'd picked a different movie, right?"

That one had also been a huge hit—but it was a horror film.

"She said when the script came her way, she just felt compelled to do it. Didn't know why. Just knew she *had* to take the part."

And Shouko understood why without him saying it aloud. It was a feeling Sakuta shared.

"I was the same way. I didn't remember anything, but the feelings remained. A vague sense I was forgetting something important, that there was something I had to do."

In his case, he'd dealt with that restless feeling by repeatedly making small donations. He didn't remember exactly when he'd started doing that, but every time he ran across a charity drive, he dumped all the change he had. Never felt the need to stop. He was still at it, consciously keeping the practice going.

He didn't think a few hundred yen would really save anyone. He didn't have anyone near him who desperately needed saving. But sometimes a lot of little things can make a difference.

Shouko being here in front of him, happily devouring her parfait? That proved it. He hadn't been able to save her—but someone else had put their name on a donor list and given her a future.

"So what brings you here today?"

Shouko took the spoon out of her mouth.

"Sakuta, have you heard of this?" she asked, pulling out her phone and showing him the screen. On it was a music video—one posted under the Touko Kirishima name.

"My sister's friend was talking about her earlier."

"You never disappoint."

"How so?"

"Destiny adores you."

"Can't say I appreciate the affections of an abstract concept."

He preferred the adorations of warmer, softer things.

"But what about this video?"

Shouko would not just be making small talk.

"Something here bugged me."

Her tone didn't change, but there was a serious glint in her eye.

"Specifically?" he said, intrigued.

"I remember *everything*."

"……"

"You and Mai might not have, but I always did. I've got several different future versions of me in here. That includes everything they knew."

That included the Shouko who'd received Sakuta's heart and the one who'd had Mai's. Possible other future Shoukos he didn't even know about.

"Mm, I knew that."

"But not this."

"Not...?"

"None of my future memories had Touko Kirishima videos in them."

"......"

Shouko was getting more serious by the second, but that wasn't what silenced him. It just took him a moment to align her words with his own experience.

"Ah, I get you now."

"Yeah."

He could see why she wasn't joking around. If none of the future Shoukos had ever seen a Touko Kirishima music video, then...she might well have existed but certainly hadn't become as popular as she was now. Something *new* was afoot. Which meant...

"The butterfly effect? You're worried that what you've done has changed the future?"

"And you're my accomplice."

Shouko shoved the last bite of parfait into her mouth. She was finally joking again.

"I don't think you need to worry about it, Makinohara."

"Because even if I'm right, and I did change someone else's life— that's *their* problem?"

That sure sounded like something he would say. And the smirk on her face looked like a kid who'd just pulled off a flawless prank. Childish, but a look the *older* Shouko had often employed.

"Yeah. I'm not so overwhelmingly nice I gotta worry about people I've never even met."

"Says the guy who drops spare change into every collection box he sees. You've got acres of unconscious kindness."

"I just couldn't think of any other way to help you."

And he was keeping it going as a way of paying the world back for saving her. Paying back not any particular person, just...the general goodwill that existed, out there somewhere.

"Either way, unless anyone's actually in *trouble*, we can let it be. If there's people who are benefiting from the changed future...well, I wouldn't mind a little of that coming my way."

At the very least, Touko Kirishima's popularity seemed like a net positive.

But his joke only elicited a hint of a smile.

"I think you've got better things to do than worry about strangers," he said.

She did.

Something far more important.

Something only Shouko could do.

He looked her right in the eye, and she smiled. Knowing what he meant.

"I've gotta enjoy life in all the ways I couldn't."

"Exactly."

"I promise I am. I mean, I could never have eaten a chocolate parfait before."

"Such a small thing."

"And the secret to true happiness is taking pleasure in the little things."

That was a very big-Shouko thing to say, and she grinned triumphantly.

"Oh yeah, that's right," he said, nodding. He glanced over at the clock. Only five minutes left. "That all you wanted to say?"

It sure sounded like she was done. But...

"Actually, there is one more thing," Shouko said. "The real reason I came to see you today."

She looked at him, seeming slightly lost. Something hard to get out? Her next words showed why.

"I'm moving away."

It didn't take much time to grasp a concept that simple.

"When? Where?"

Sakuta knew right away what to ask.

"Tomorrow, ten AM flight…to Okinawa."

"That's sudden."

Well, it was to him. Maybe not to her.

"Warm weather takes less of a toll on me," she said, looking more relaxed.

"School?"

"I've still got junior high classes…but we're gonna use March to settle in, and I'll be back in school in the new year."

"Oh."

"Mai kept it secret, then?"

"Huh?"

"I sent her a letter last week. Advanced warning."

"Yeah?"

"And I asked her to take care of you."

"And she answered?"

"It came this morning."

She took a blue envelope out of her bag.

To Sakuta, this was his first love and his current love, and he wasn't really sure he wanted to know what they were talking about.

But he felt like not asking would make this parting worse.

"What'd she say?"

"When we're settled in, she'll bring you down to hang out."

"Oh."

"Mm."

"To Okinawa… Sounds nice."

"I'll write you once I get my bearings."

"Looking forward to it. If you take any good pictures, send those along."

"I'll be sure to include some nosebleed-inducing swimsuit shots."

"You'll need to wait at least three years for that."

"Then I take 'em. Start a big fight with Mai when you least expect it."

"Can't wait."

"Good."

Shouko gave him her nicest smile. It was blinding. And Sakuta did his best to sear that into his memory.

Okinawa was a short flight away. It was part of Japan, a lot more accessible than the past or the future.

But it would be a while before he saw Shouko smile again.

And he'd miss that. Obviously. But he didn't say so. Shouko had conquered her condition and had her whole life ahead of her. Moving was the first step to that. So...

"Makinohara."

"Yes?"

"Get out there and knock 'em dead."

He held out a hand.

"I will," she said, wrapping her little hand around it.

4

A plane flying across a clear blue sky.

The sky over the ocean.

Over the horizon.

From here, the plane's flight seemed devoid of sound.

On the beach at Shichirigahama, Sakuta could only hear the wind and the surf.

"Makinohara should be in Okinawa by now."

Yesterday at the restaurant, Shouko had said her flight was at ten. He didn't have a watch with him, so he wasn't sure what time it was, but judging by the rumbling in his belly, it was probably nearly one.

Today, Sakuta had come to the Minegahara graduation ceremony— which started at the same time her flight left. It was the remaining students' job to see the third-years out.

The ceremony had gone smoothly and wrapped up on schedule— just before noon.

There'd been a lengthy milling-about phase before they got the go-ahead to leave; when a teacher finally told them to disperse, it was half past twelve.

Sakuta had left school, but rather than head home, he'd come down to the beach.

Not basking in the sentimentality of the ceremony or anything—he still had a whole year of high school ahead of him. And didn't have enough attachment to school to have any feels in the first place. Not yet, anyway.

Mai had graduated, but that didn't seem like a big deal. At best, he'd woken up going, "Last day to see her in uniform!"

No, he'd come down to the beach because, on the train to school, Mai had said they should meet here once it was over.

And Mai wasn't here yet.

As he waited, the plane grew smaller. Carrying someone off to the other side of the sky.

Shouko wasn't on *this* plane, but he watched it go until the vapor trails faded.

When those were gone, he took a long scan of the sea, from right to left.

This was where he'd met Shouko.

She'd been the older version then.

A few more years, and "Makinohara" would be the age "Shouko" had been. He just had to wait, and he could see her again.

The idea struck him as funny, and he started laughing.

Laughter and good times. Warm feelings.

He felt like they'd look back on everything they'd been through and laugh about how crazy it had all been. That was a future worth looking forward to.

Even as that thought crossed his mind, he heard footsteps on the sand behind him.

He hoped it was Mai, but the steps were too light, the distance between them too short. He was still frowning about that when the corner of his eye caught a tiny figure.

A little girl with a red leather backpack, slipping past him. Red scarf trailing behind.

She went down to the surf, standing just beyond the wave's reach.

Beautiful, perfectly straight, shoulder-length black hair. The backpack looked brand-new, with not a scratch or stain on it.

She was probably six or seven years old.

Sakuta didn't know her.

But he'd caught a glimpse of her face in profile, and it looked just like Mai had as a child actress.

And that realization felt very wrong. A strong sense of déjà vu.

This exact thing had happened to him before.

Or rather, he'd dreamed about it.

But this was no dream.

It was real.

So what *was* this?

His head filled with questions.

And hoping for answers, he called out, "Mai?"

The girl turned, hair swaying.

A defensive look in her eyes. She looked right at Sakuta.

"Who are you, mister?" she asked, her tone bright and childlike.

The same thing she'd said in the dream.

Afterword

New plots going.
  Anime production moving.
  Look forward to new volumes and more news.

I'd like to extend a special thanks to all students and faculty members of the high school who answered the questions I had while writing this.

Keji Mizoguchi, Araki from editorial, Fujiwara, Kurokawa, Kurosaki—you were all a huge help.

I hope we'll all meet again next time, in Volume 9.

Hajime Kamoshida